THE
RETURN

THE CHRONICLES OF
THE DOOR

Gene Edwards

Tyndale House
Publishers, Inc.
Wheaton, Illinois

Library of Congress Cataloging-in-Publication Data

Edwards, Gene, date
   The return / Gene Edwards.
       p.   cm. — (The chronicles of the door)
      ISBN 0-8423-5601-0 (alk. paper)
      1. Bible. N.T.—History of Biblical events—Fiction. I. Title.
  II. Series: Edwards, Gene, 1932–   Chronicles of the door.
  PS3555.D924R48   1996
  813′.54—dc20   95-26636

Printed in the United States of America

02 01 00 99 98 97 96
7   6   5   4   3   2

PROLOGUE

"Houston, this is Hubble Seven."

"Come in, Hubble Seven."

"Houston, we've got a . . . some sort of space anomaly out here."

"A what?"

"Well, it's . . ."

"Just a moment, Hubble."

"Hello, Houston. This is Jet Propulsion Laboratories."

"Pasadena, come in."

"We're getting some strange readings from the Venusian and Martian orbiting platforms."

"What is it, JPL?"

"Well, it's rather hard to describe. I'm not sure."

"Houston, this is Freedom Platform Nine."

"Come in, Freedom."

"Our onboard radioscope—we turned it on the area Hubble Seven is looking at. We're getting some rather unusual readings, Houston. We are not sure what it is we have, but there is some sort of problem. At least it seems that way. First a strong burst of—"

"Just a moment, Freedom. I've got communications coming in from four, five space stations. Hubble, hold. Everyone seems to be reporting in on the same thing, I think. Everyone hold! You folks are really messing up a beautiful autumn day.

"OK, we are tying all of you together. Stay on the line. Now, would everyone please feed us the coordinates you have of this anomaly. Maybe we can find its position and make some sense out of all this. If any of you get any new information, pass it on to us here in Houston. We'll pass it on to everyone else."

"This is Hubble Seven. Houston, I think we have the clearest look at this thing."

"All right, Hubble, report."

"The best that we can tell . . . Houston, we're not sure—you know we have never seen anything like this. Shucks, we've never *heard* of anything like this. Anyway, it looks like some sort of tear in space."

"What!"

"Yeah. A tear in space."

"Hubble Seven, would you wake up the Pluto satellite. As best we can tell from what all of you have sent us, the Pluto satellite is on the other side of the anomaly. Let's get a backside view."

"Hubble here. We're feeding in coordinates to the Pluto telescope now. It's turning in that direction. We'll get a backside view of this anomaly any moment now."

"Anything new, Freedom?"

"Yeah! Sweat!"

"Houston, this is Hubble Seven again. I think we have a bit of a problem. A historic one."

"What is it, Hubble?"

"Well, after I tell you this, I'm prepared to turn in my resignation on the ground of being unfit to serve."

"I think we all are, Hubble. What do you have?"

"Our scope is seeing *lights*. Lights! They seem to be *inside* the tear."

"It has an inside?"

"It sure looks like it."

"Inside?"

"Yeah. It's like we're looking into the tear, and something is going on *inside*."

"What?"

"Well, what we're seeing is flashing lights, sort of like meteors, passing back and forth."

"Inside the tear, you see lights moving back and forth? As they pass the tear, you see them flash by. Is that it?"

"Yeah. You think maybe we're all going crazy up here?"

"Check your oxygen levels. Maybe you're getting too much space juice. Are the lights coming *out* of the tear?"

"No, they're passing back and forth. Boy, do they move rapidly."

"How rapidly?"

"We're not sure. We'll give you a reading in just a moment."

"Are you getting anything from the Pluto telescope?"

"Yeah, we sent it to JPL for decoding."

"JPL, this is Houston. What do you have?"

"This is JPL. We're getting data now. It's not good."

"What have you got, JPL?"

"Maybe *my* resignation. Any chance we've all gone bats?"

"JPL, report. Resign later."

"You're not going to believe this, Houston. We are getting absolutely *nothing!* That Pluto telescope is looking right at the backside of those coordinates, and it does not see *anything.* From Pluto's view it's just ordinary space."

"All right, I'll toss it on the table. Anybody got any ideas? You're all seeing some sort of anomaly, but Pluto is on the other side of it, and from the backside there is nothing!

"A little louder, fellas!"

"This is JPL. We're all busy writing our resignations."

"This is Hubble Seven. Isn't it obvious? We're looking through a tear into another universe . . . or another realm . . . or another world . . . or another continuum. If we were in a spacecraft and swung around to the backside of that tear, we wouldn't see it. We are looking at another world with another dimension."

"A black hole?"

"Naw, black holes don't have shooting lights. *An-*

other realm. This tear has revealed another creation we did not know about. There's another world on the other side of that tear, Houston. At least, that's the way Hubble sees it."

"This is JPL. We tend to concur. Houston, maybe it's time to notify the president."

"Yes! I thought about that. But what is he going to do? Call out the marines?!"

"Uh-oh, this is Hubble Seven again. We've got more problems than we thought."

"What are you seeing, Hubble?"

"We're seeing a very bright light. It's behind the tear."

"How bright?"

"Houston, we don't know. We'll try to get some measurements on it, but I am not sure our instruments are going to be able to register this. It is a *lot* brighter than the sun."

"Wh—! Somebody get me Chris Johnson in here, and get him in here fast."

"Who?"

"Chris Johnson."

"You mean the jani—the custodian?!"

"No, I mean Chris Johnson, the assistant building engineer."

"Yes, sir."

"Have you got any readings there, Hubble?"

"No, but I can tell you this. It *is* a very bright light, and it seems to be moving toward . . . I think we've got more problems, Houston. *Big* ones!"

"What is it, Hubble? Hello, Chris."

"Yes, sir."

"Chris, look over at that monitor. What do you see?"

"Uh, I'm not sure, sir. Where is that?"

"It's up in the sky above the earth, and . . . "

"Houston, this is Hubble Seven, and this is important."

"Chris, what you see on that screen is from the telescope onboard Hubble Seven. But it's soon going to become visible to the naked eye. Every eye on this side of the planet will soon be able to see that light. It's getting brighter and brighter."

"Houston, this is Hubble Seven. I'm telling you, listen to me! Houston, we've got *the* view on this. We are seeing things you can't. There's not just one light. There are many. But the brightest is central. It's moving toward the tear, maybe through it . . . coming this way. The other lights, much smaller, not as bright, they seem . . . are you ready for this? They seem to be forming into some sort of . . . formation."

"Out in front of the brightest light?"

"No, they are falling into formation behind the bright light."

"Chris, what do you think? React!"

"Why are you asking me? I'm no astronomer."

"No, Chris, you're not. But you are a very religious man. Have you got any idea what that is?"

"Well, sir, yes. I think . . ."

"Hello, Houston. This is Hubble Seven again. You

should definitely notify the president. I think every space platform and major telescope in existence should be let in on this."

"Yeah, the phones are starting to ring off the wall. We are going to need all the info we can get, and give."

"Hello, Houston. This is Mount Palomar. We've got something very unusual going on here."

"Mount Palomar, what have you got?!"

"Well, that tear; we're plotting the light. It *is* moving! Fast! It's moving through the tear into our realm, *right now.*"

"Houston, this is Hubble Seven. The more we look at this, it doesn't look like a tear at all. It looks like . . . I don't want to say this . . . it looks like . . . well, a door, a *very* big . . . *door.*"

"Chris, what do you think of this?"

"Hello, Houston. This is JPL. We've got something very strange."

"What was that? An earthquake? Has Houston, Texas, ever had an earthquake? Houston doesn't have earthquakes. This whole place is shaking."

"Houston, listen to us. This is JPL. Our audio spectrometers and echographs, they're registering some sort of gigantic sound wave emanating from out of the tear. Earth cannot hear it yet, but, boy, you're gonna hear it. It's moving toward earth at the speed of sound. Not light. Brace yourselves, that shaking you felt is nothing but space giving way to a very large sound shield headed our way. Earth is about to get its first *soundquake.* Man, what I'd give to be on Jupiter right now."

"Wouldn't we all, Pasadena."

"How loud is it, JPL?"

"Well, the phrase 'loud enough to wake the dead' comes to mind!"

"Uh-oh! Houston, either we're nuts and all our instruments have gone crazy, or earth just speeded up its rotation."

"What?"

"This is Hubble. We can see it and measure it. JPL is correct! Everybody on earth is gonna see that thing out there. Soon! This planet is moving fast enough to rip out of orbit."

"Houston, you might as well know this. Most of the folks here at JPL have asked to go home to their families."

"Chris?"

"Yes, sir?"

"Have you anything to say to us all-wise rocket scientists?"

"Yes, sir."

"What do you think this is? Do you have any idea?"

"No, sir, I don't think. I *know!*"

"What is it, Chris?"

"Sir, it's *The Return!*"

PART

I

CHAPTER
One

"Prisoner, you have caused this council great distress. We have had much discussion concerning what to do with you.

"Others of your kin came here years ago, spreading your new religion. It was a grave mistake that we allowed them to live among us, making converts of our people.

"The year your temple was destroyed by the armies of Rome and your capital city was leveled, you and other Hebrews fled here, joining yourself to the secret gatherings of this sect here in Asia Minor.

"Now our all-wise Emperor Domitian has seen your evil and has commanded that all of you be wiped off the earth.

"Hear, then, the final judgment of this council concerning your fate.

In the fortieth year of the reign of our god and lord, the Emperor Domitian, the Council of Ephesus, acting on behalf of the laws of Caesar Domitian and those of the Empire, do hereby sentence one John of Galilee, a

fisherman, to exile upon the island of Patmos in the Aegean Sea, there to remain until his death.

The Hebrew's crime is that of refusing to cast incense into the flame that burns upon the altar of the temple of the god Domitian.

John, having openly confessed to this crime, shall be removed from Ephesus and from this province on the morrow and taken to Patmos.

In exiling this old man, it is hoped that the followers of his teachings will disperse or return to the gods of Rome.

"Take the prisoner. See that he is on his way to Patmos by daybreak. Never let him see this place again, unless it is in the temple, paying homage to the gods."

CHAPTER
Two

"It is agreed then."

The voice was that of Epaphras.

"We will send seven men, under cover of night, to Patmos. They will report to John the gravity of the conditions here in Ephesus and the surrounding area, as well as pass on reports of the situation in Italy, North Africa, and Galatia. John will also be presented with the questions we have drawn up here tonight, in hopes that he will respond by means of a letter addressed to the churches in Asia Minor."

"Epaphras, a question."

"Yes?"

"I believe we have overlooked one matter. John is near ninety years of age. I doubt he can see well enough to write. Ought we not send an amanuensis with the seven messengers?"

"*An* amanuensis or *the* amanuensis?" responded Epaphras.

A ripple of laughter crossed the room. "It just so happens that Tertius of Corinth is visiting among us."

"Tertius, are you willing? There is danger."

"I have written three letters to Nero and one to Domitian in my lifetime. Is there more to fear?" remonstrated Tertius.

"Are your eyes as keen as when you wrote for Paul?"

"No, but I make up for it with a broader stroke."

"It is time, then, to select the seven messengers who will make this journey to Patmos. If a letter comes to us from John, let it be quickly carried to all seven regions of Asia Minor. Rome has provided us with a great circular road that binds the seven regions together; therefore, we need to select someone from the north, another from the northeast, another from the Hermus valley. Then there is the area around Lydia. Though there is but one gathering in the region, someone from Philadelphia needs also to be selected. Also, there is the Lycus valley. Someone from the brothers and sisters in the region of north Ionia, where there is only the gathering in the city of Smyrna. And, of course, here in Ephesus for all the lower Maeander valley and the west."

By the time night had fallen, seven messengers from the seven regions of Asia Minor had been selected to sail to Patmos. With them a man gifted in writing very swiftly, the amanuensis Tertius.

Unknown to them, these eight were about to become part of a journey that would never be forgotten as long as the species of man would live upon the earth.

CHAPTER
Three

"Are you sure? There are many islands in the Sporades. Besides, the morning light is still quite dim."

"True, but only Patmos has those white crags along its shoreline. Nor are any of the other islands in the Sporades so barren, rocky, and desolate."

"Can you be equally sure of the proper place for landing?"

"What is that!"

"Someone on shore, waving."

"It is John. I would know that silhouette anywhere."

"Row with your hearts, brothers."

"He is wading out into the water!"

"Should a man his age be doing that?"

"He was born to the sea. I doubt he could do any other and keep conscience with himself. The waters are part of his life."

"When the boat bottoms, move quickly; and as quickly find a place to hide the boat."

"Welcome, brothers!" called John.

"John, careful!"

"I received the message of your coming. You have nothing to fear. Romans are not frequently in this area. How good it is to have you. This way. But slowly, these eyes do not see as well as once they did.

"Follow this path. It leads to my cave."

"You live in a cave?"

"Not exactly. It is really the mouth of an ancient mine, abandoned over a century ago. The mines on this side of Patmos are all exhausted. All the present mining going on is centered some fifty miles from here, on the far side of the island.

"Here, sit at the cave's entrance; it is better that way. I was told you would be seven. I see eight!"

"We also brought an amanuensis."

"Tertius, old friend!"

"John!"

"Now, let me guess why they sent you. Would I be far from the mark if I assumed that bag was filled with pens, ink, and unused scrolls?"

"Not far at all, John," replied the good-natured scribe.

The face of John grew sober.

"You have come here for good reason, I am sure. It does not go well in Asia Minor, does it?"

"John, the assembled ones in Italy are being ravaged, many are dead, more are in prison. In North Africa it is the same. Every gathering in Greece is under the full fury of Rome. Galatia fares no better. But the brothers and sisters in Asia Minor suffer the most. There are no gatherings except in the dead of night, and only then with the greatest of caution. The situation is very grim wherever Rome reigns."

John's eyes shined with mist, his forehead furrowed, but his only response was silence, and a tear.

After several minutes, he spoke.

"What is it that you ask of me? A letter, perhaps?"

"John, anything. There are so many questions, and no answers. The brothers and sisters have requested that we present you with a few of these questions in the hope that you will respond. Yes, hopefully, in written word, so that we might pass your letter out among the assemblies. Perhaps all we really ask is a word of comfort."

"It is a quirk of man to credit old age with wisdom it does not possess," answered John. "I have no idea what to say.

"But come, let us dine. We will speak more of these matters."

"John, uh, there is something we all want to ask you. In light of the present situation, well, there is a legend."

John straightened. "Ah, that about Peter, and what the Lord said to him about my death. Yes, let us speak of that."

CHAPTER
Four

"We were in Galilee. Peter and I were with the Lord, beside the shore. He had spoken to us of many things. Then his words to Peter seemed to indicate how Peter would die.

"Hearing that, Peter asked the Lord how *I* would die!"

A mischievous smile crossed John's face.

"Perhaps Peter was hoping I would be present to die with him. Peter's words were, 'Lord, what of this man?' . . . pointing at me. The Lord replied to Peter, 'What is it to you if I desire that he be remaining while I am coming?'"

John paused, and his face lightened.

"I have no idea what the Lord meant. None!"

The old man leaned back to observe his eight companions.

No one responded.

"There is something I do know," he continued, warming to his subject. *"I know why you asked this question!* You hope it means I will be alive when the Lord returns to earth to claim his own."

John paused again, a broad smile breaking across his face. "If that be true, it also means none of you will have to die!"

The cave resounded with laughter.

"We have been caught," admitted Tertius.

"Everyone, it seems, wants the Lord to come while they are alive. That way they would not have to die. Such hopes give birth to wild speculation."

"Then you have no idea when the Lord will return?"

"None. I would remind you that the Son does not know. It is a matter reserved only to the Father. But," sighed John, "I doubt that fact will prevent anyone from guessing."

"John, this is one of the questions we have been asked to present to you. Will the faith survive Domitian? Will any be left alive at the Lord's return, or will he come only to call forth those who are dead?"

John folded his hands, stared into the cave's darkness, then replied almost in a whisper. "Imagine the intimacy, the oneness of the Father and Son; yet the Father has concealed this one mystery, keeping it for himself alone. If the Lord Jesus were sitting here among us at this moment, he would know no more than I. *He does not know.*

"If I say to you, 'I hope' or 'I *think* that will be,' or if I say, 'It looks like the end,' that would not make it the end. We all wish to know, but until something new is bequeathed to me, I know nothing beyond these words:

He will descend
with
a shout,
the dead in Christ
will rise,
then those who
are alive
will meet him
in the air.

"I believe there will be many believers when he comes. It matters not what Domitian or any other man or nation does. But again, I must say to you, *I* do not know."

"We must tell you, John, the believers all over the Empire live in constant fear. There are many questions and some doubtings. If you would write to the churches words of comfort, we will copy your letter and see that it is passed out across the empire."

"You are from seven churches?"

"Yes."

"What cities?"

"Ephesus, Pergamum, Laodicea, Philadelphia, Sardis, Smyrna, and Thyatira."

"Ah, from all seven regions! What do you want me to write?"

"Anything! You are the sole survivor of the Twelve. *Anything* would be received with great appreciation."

"A letter that would resolve all the questions of all men concerning the Lord's ways and the Lord's com-

ing," answered John dryly, his wit discernible only in his sparkling eyes.

"John, perhaps we are expecting too much, but still, will you write a letter?"

"Hhhmmm!

"It is my custom on the Lord's Day to rise early and mount the nearby hill, which I am sure you saw. Tomorrow, before the dawn, I will climb the hill; there I will bring this matter before my Lord. Let us hope he gives me some wisdom concerning your request.

"When I return, because it is the Lord's Day, let us break bread and celebrate our Lord."

PART

II

CHAPTER
Five

"Did you hear?! The Door. It has moved to a hill on Patmos. John is on his way up the hill—now!" exclaimed an angel named Exalta, a bit more excited than angels are supposed to be.

"It has been a long time since someone from *their* realm has visited *ours!*" rejoined his companion Rathel.

"Will he actually come here, or only look into our realm?" wondered Exalta out loud.

"Michael stands at the Door now, as intent as ever I have seen him. Let us join him."

Michael, standing just inside heaven's portal, was watching an old man trudging up the side of a hill. "John's back is to us, but in a few moments he will turn. When he does, he will see," said Michael to himself.

"How many of the sons of mankind has the Lord allowed to see the heavenlies?"

Michael turned to face his inquisitor.

"Rathel! Exalta!"

The question posed to Michael intrigued him as much as it had the two curious angels.

"First, of course, was Adam. He moved in and out of our realm at will, as we did his. Then Enoch . . . and Abraham. After that, the memorable night spent with Jacob. Moses . . . several times. He and the seventy elders actually dined here! Then David . . . he was allowed to see the Holy of Holies, even as was Moses.

"But there was nothing like the visit of Isaiah. Now *there* was an hour never to be forgotten."

"Agreed," responded Exalta. "The entire heavenly host surrounded the throne, joined by seraphim and cherubim."

"Can a mortal see the resurrected Lord in unveiled glory and live? Or will the sight alone strike him dead? Frail mortality was never constructed to survive such a sight, was it?" asked Rathel.

"For better or worse, we shall know soon enough," continued Michael, as he turned back toward the Door just in time to see John arrive at the crest of the hill.

"Recorder has sought to explain something to me, but it is beyond my spirit to grasp," mused Michael.

Exalta and Rathel leaned forward.

"John may be allowed to see the future. It may be that he will see *us* . . . in the future. Then, in some distant hour, we may see John watching us! We will have finally caught up with what he will have already seen!"

"I join you, Michael. Neither do I grasp such a

word," agreed Exalta. "If he sees the future, does that mean he will be allowed to see—"

"The Return?" interrupted Rathel.

Michael was about to reply when he was interrupted by the voice of a mortal.

"Lord . . ."

It was John. He was looking out over the Icarian Sea, watching the sun rise in its glory, unaware that a far greater glory stood behind him.

"We must depart this place at once," ordered Michael. "This moment is for the Lord and John, and no other."

As the angels disappeared, the Lord approached, taking his place at the Door, just behind John.

"Lord . . . ," whispered John again.

CHAPTER
Six

Watching the golden sun rise above the horizon of the sparkling sea, John devotedly whispered his Lord's name from time to time.

After a long while, he began to speak.

So much to know
yet little known.
Darkness holds the hour;
loose upon the earth
its power.
Fourscore and ten my years;
never
have I seen so many
tears.
She who was born
from out your riven
side—
Can your bride
long this hour
abide?
A monster sits

> *on seven hills;*
> *imprisons, tramples*
> *kills.*
> *My brothers bid me*
> *write,*
> *seeking comfort*
> *seeking light.*
>
> *Wisdom is not mine*
> *but thine.*
> *Empty words*
> *I dare not write.*
> *Give to me*
> *Lord*
> *words of light.*
> *One thing*
> *and*
> *this alone I need:*
> *Your face*
> *to sight*
> *then shall*
> *I boldly write.*

John fell silent, but soon a sense began to grow inside him that there was someone else present.

John raised one hand toward the skies. "I know that presence, and know you well." He closed his eyes and waited.

The winds of the Aegean Sea began to blow furiously; then, just as suddenly, all sound and sense grew eerily still. John was gripped with the feeling that the entire world had vanished and that he was standing upon a threshold of nothingness.

"Can that be?"

Even as John uttered those words, his mind flashed back to past scenes: a Door in heaven, and a voice calling out, "This is my beloved Son"; then a scene of Mount Tabor, of an enveloping cloud; a room in Jerusalem, tightly locked; a small second-story chamber and the sound of a rushing wind.

"Have I come to another hour as momentous as those? Or is this but the longing of an old man's imagination? After all, old men *do* dream dreams."

Wanting very much to open his eyes, John realized he lacked the courage to do so.

A mighty thunderclap changed that.

"No imagination is this," resolved John as he heard the peal of ten thousand blaring trumpets.

"This is real!"

Then came a most recognizable voice, one as familiar to him as his own.

John!

CHAPTER
Seven

John forced open one eye. Before him, *nothing*. He looked down. His feet were resting on the edge of an abyss of an endless void.

"Where is he," came John's panicked words. "There is nothing . . . anywhere." A thought exploded in his mind. "Behind me. He is behind me!"

Again John heard that voice.

"Write.

"Write what you see. Send *my* letter to the seven messengers and to the seven gatherings."

In terror that was mingled with joy, John whirled about. And in doing so he saw his Lord. Dazzling light, terrifying sights, overpowering symbols, and a kaleidoscope of compressed time followed.

Later that day, John would try to describe with the inadequacy of words that which met his eyes when he turned.

I

saw

seven menorah lampstands,

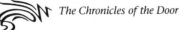

> *and*
>
> *in the midst of those seven menorahs*
> *I*
> *saw*
> *my Lord*
> *revealing himself*
> *in*
> *unrestrained*
> *glory.*
> *The instant I saw him*
> *I died—*
> *or so I thought,*
> *for*
> *I fell at his feet*
> *as one struck dead*
> *by unapproachable light.*

A torrent of words issuing from the Son of Man rushed over John. He recalled only one thought that was his own, "Thank God that it is not I who will write to the assemblies. My Lord writes to them. Better, far better, than any words which man might pen."

Words from his Lord continued to flood John, drowning his mind in sights and images that seared themselves into John's very being.

At last the words came to an end. The Lord had finished speaking to the seven messengers.

Hesitantly John raised his head, then pushed him-

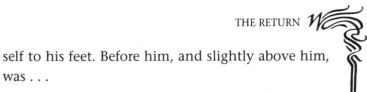

self to his feet. Before him, and slightly above him, was . . .

The Door

To John's amazement, and contrary to the record of the first book of Moses, the Door was neither closed nor guarded. The Door was open. Wide open. "How can that be? Open! Dare man pass through that Door to other realms?" A voice gave answer by way of command. "John, come! Step through the Door!"

*Come into the
other realm,
and I will show you
what must come to pass.*

Instantly John found himself in the habitat of angels.

"I do not belong here," he found himself muttering. "This is not where man should tread. I am the most alien of aliens in this place."

*The throne,
the supernal place,
glistens like a diamond
turned to fire.
Around about,
a storm*

35

> *whirling*
> *bright,*
> *bursting in every shade*
> *of*
> *emerald's light.*
> *Even angels dare not*
> *this space.*

"Write! How shall I write? No mortal, nor immortal, can find the pen to scribe such wonder," pleaded John. "I cannot see these things and live. My grave shall be beside the throne."

At that moment an angel came to John and ushered him into the sights of history *now,* history *soon,* and history *future,* his journey culminating in the presence of the grandest pageantry the eyes of God and men shall ever see.

At last the vision ended. A man almost mad, yet never saner, rushed down Patmos's hill shouting, "A pen, give to me a pen! For I must write or I must die."

CHAPTER
Eight

"Quickly!" thundered the old man. "Where is Tertius? Find me Tertius!"

John's eyes swarmed with heaven's glow, his face alive with light, but his clothes were bedraggled and drenched in sweat.

"John, you look awful!"

"Perhaps, but never have I felt better. Tertius, your pen. Now! At that table. Now! All the rest of you—out. Out now. Out! I will call you when I am done. Do you hear? Out with you."

The seven men might have been frightened or even offended at other times, but the radiance of John's face told them this was no ordinary hour—nor was it the time for human things, such as words and feelings. Obediently they rushed from the cave, but paused not too far distant in hopes of hearing something of John's continuing verbosity.

"I think he's decided to write the letter!" laughed one.

John, in the meantime, was babbling his way back to normality.

"Tertius, I was wrong. I was very wrong."

"What?" responded a bemused Tertius.

"A letter I wrote not long ago, the short one. It has been copied and sent . . . everywhere, but I was wrong in what I wrote. What I said was this, 'We do not know what we shall be like . . .'"

"Oh, that!" exclaimed Tertius. You said, 'We know not what we shall be, but we shall be like him.'"

"Yes, yes! And I was wrong! *Now* I know. I know *what* we shall be like! I saw him, Tertius, I saw my Lord . . . as he *is*. Not like unto the Lord I knew in Galilee. Nor even the Lord I knew after he rose from the grave. No, I saw him as he is *now!* As he *really* is. And we . . . we shall be . . . we shall be like *that!*"

John darted about from one end of the cave to the other, ranting as he moved.

"Remember! I must remember it all!"

Tertius was furiously unrolling a scroll. As he dipped his pen into awaiting ink, he exclaimed, "Now, John, now!"

"Lord," cried John. "Give this Hebrew mind the gift to speak in Greek!

"Tertius! Write! When we finish, copy. There dare not be only one record of this, lest the Romans destroy it. And pray that I do not die before these things are inscribed.

"Is there ink enough? And several quills, and papyrus? How shall I begin, Tertius?"

"Uh . . ."

"Can I tell men what I have seen? Neither mind

nor word nor pen of man is endowed with so grand a gift. But I must try. I must write to the assemblies. I must haste, for I dare not forget. Now, you must be careful to make it clear that whereas the Lord's people in the gatherings have asked me to write them, it is not I who writes. It is the Lord himself. He has written to the seven assemblies. He has spoken to them, and to me, of many things. You and I will put it on parchment, but it is the Lord whose words we place there."

"Who . . . what did you see?"

"What did I see! What did I really see? I saw Jesus Christ *revealed!* Yes. And that is how we shall begin this letter.

The revelation of Jesus Christ, which God has given to him that he might show to his bondservant, John.

And so John began. For hours he spoke, and for hours Tertius faithfully wrote. Toward evening the writing was finished. Outside, seven messengers had not moved from the cave's entrance.

"We are finished, Tertius."

"But, John, no! You left something out. When you got to the seventh thunder, you didn't tell what the seventh thunder said. What did the seventh thunder say?" probed a frustrated Tertius.

John laughed.

"Tertius, you are the first of what will probably be many men who will ask, 'What did the seventh

thunder say?' Yes, there were seven thunders. Six of them my Lord told me I could record. I was allowed to tell what I saw and heard. But what the seventh thunder said? I was told by my Lord that I was not to record what I heard.

"Sorry, my brother, but the seventh thunder resides with me alone, and perhaps dies with me alone."

"Did you find out if the Lord is coming? Is this the end? And if it is . . ."

"Tertius! Quiet! Until someone besides me knows what is in the seventh thunder, no man will ever know anything of certainty about the *time* of the Lord's return. What the seventh thunder said, I *will not tell*. Any man who speaks of when my Lord will return, without the seventh thunder, is a man given to great foolishness.

"I have seen much, and you have recorded some portion thereof. All except the seventh thunder. Be content, Tertius. You now know as much as I do. *Almost!*

"And remember, my curious friend, even the Son of God knows not the day nor hour. If some foolish believer feels he can unravel this vision and discover what neither the Lord nor I know—he would be wise to remember that one-seventh of this book is missing," continued John in a voice of quiet satisfaction.

"A seventh?" sighed an incredulous Tertius.

"John, what have you learned this day?" came Tertius's meek inquiry.

"At this moment I have only what I already had: the hope of his return. But surely what has been written will be of great comfort to the persecuted ones. One thing is certain, the faith *will not* be trampled out by Domitian. Our Lord, his people . . . *will* triumph. Tertius, be of this assurance:

He will return!

"Now call the seven messengers. Is there any among them who can read? If so, I will ask him to read the scroll out loud. You and I shall listen."

"And answer their questions!" laughed Tertius.

"One last thing, Tertius. We must have a number of copies of this book. Perhaps we need a word of warning at the end to discourage anyone who makes a copy from adding or leaving out any of its contents."

Tertius's eyes twinkled. "I've something in mind!"

"Good! Now call the seven messengers. Tell them I have a letter to the assemblies. I *do* have a letter. Indeed, I do!"

PART

III

CHAPTER
Nine

"Recorder, because you were the first of my creation, you will be the first to hear. My return to earth draws near."

"At last, man shall own his king," replied Recorder in grand relief.

"Lord, is it true that you have not known until now?"

"No one has . . . until now. Only my Father. Nonetheless, Recorder, you do not seem too surprised."

"My Lord, on the day you presented to me the Book of Records, all pages were blank. Since that day I have inscribed all events of heaven and earth. But now there is left but *one* page!"

The Lord responded with laughter. "Then write well, Recorder, for the hour of all hours approaches. Soon even the last page will be filled. Then, no more, forever!"

"May I inquire of you this question, Lord? What event has transpired that has made possible your return?"

"Only that it is my Father's good pleasure!"

"That simple. Ah! So much waste in all our specu-
lations."

"Now, Recorder, it is time for two of your companions to know these matters."

At that moment Gabriel appeared.

"I sensed your call, Lord."

"I also," said Michael, appearing but an instant
later.

"Michael," came Recorder's stern voice, "be prepared
to restrain yourself. You are about to hear of . . ."

"The Return!" exclaimed Michael. "I knew it. I felt
it!"

"As I said, Michael . . ."

"You are concerned about me," rebuffed Michael.
"What of all the other angels? What will happen
when they hear? Recorder, I am one; they are millions."

"Lord, it is true?" asked Gabriel.

"It is."

"Wonder of wonders! But I must agree with
Michael. How shall we contain ourselves when we
see you descend, and when we see the redeemed
ones break forth into the skies, and when . . ."

"Why should you contain yourselves?" replied the
Lord. Then, pointing at Gabriel's side, he continued.

"Your trumpet, Gabriel!"

"My trumpet, Lord?"

"How long has it been at your side?"

"Since my beginning, Lord."

"You have sounded it?"

"Only on the rarest occasions."

"And . . . ?"

". . . with the greatest of restraint and caution, lest I shatter creation."

The Lord's eyes blazed. "No more caution, Gabriel."

Gabriel began to shake. "Never have I been so close to unbelief," he choked.

"Michael, your sword."

Before the Lord's words were completed, Michael's sword was fully drawn and poised above his head.

"You have made much use of your sword, Michael?"

"Oft," came the cool voice of Michael, his eyes reflecting the fire in the eyes of his Lord.

"Ever to its fullest?"

"I dare not, Lord, lest I split a universe."

"No more restraint, Michael. For today is *the Day. The Day of the Lord.*"

Tears poured across the faces of the two archangels.

"The Day of the Lord. The Day of the Lord," Michael repeated again and again.

"But still I must ask, how shall I announce these things to the heavenly host?" repeated Gabriel. "We shall not finish our words before chaos reigns!"

"Then let chaos reign!" replied the Lord. "This is *not* a solemn moment! Nor is it an hour for caution.

"Come. Stand with me before the open Door."

"Now, Lord?!"

"Now!"

The Door began to move, and as it did, the heavens began to shake.

"The Door never seemed so vast, nor has it ever opened upon this particular place," observed Michael quietly. "Between the sixth and seventh planets?" he whispered. "What a view of the bright blue ball!"

"What a vantage point!" exuded a wide-eyed Gabriel.

"Yes," replied Recorder, "for us, as we look down. And . . ."

"And for earth, as they look *up!*" interjected Michael.

"Ready yourself to receive your Lord, O earth!" said Gabriel almost inaudibly. "No more caution! Trumpet, at last, you shall find your true recoil!" he blustered.

"No more restraint," echoed Michael.

"Now, Gabriel! Bring the heavenly host. *All* of them, for we descend. *Now!*"

CHAPTER
Ten

"Come from the far reaches of galaxies; come from all heavenly places, comrades of the eternals," commanded Gabriel.

Like stars in fiery flight, fifty million messengers of God swarmed before the Door and came to formation behind Gabriel. Intoxicated with excitement, they roared their enthusiasm as they watched fifty million more rampaging angels appear and fall into formation behind Michael.

Gabriel knew it now fell to him to proclaim to the awaiting angels the grand news, but for the first time ever he was utterly at a loss as to how to begin. It was a proclamation destined never to be delivered, for at that instant the Lord stepped onto the threshold of the Door; behind him, in full view, the fallen planet.

Michael grabbed Gabriel's arm. "Say nothing, or there will be a complete loss of what little order there is. Look at their eyes. They *know!*"

Without a word, Gabriel rushed to the front of his charge and raised his trumpet high above his head.

With that, the entire angelic host exploded with shouts of joy!

Michael could control himself no more. "This is *the* hour," he exclaimed as he unsheathed the mightiest sword in creation. At the sight of that incomparable weapon, one hundred million swords lifted above the heads of the army of God, even as a victory cry rose from their throats.

"Every messenger to his station. Every angel to his charge," ordered Gabriel. "Mankind has always had heavenly guardians. Today they shall see their guardians. When they do, let them understand the protecting and sovereign hand of their God. Let them see you as you are, mighty and strong. But most of all, let them know to whom we, their guardians, owe our allegiance."

"Look to the Door!" exclaimed Recorder. "It has moved. It is exactly level with earth's equator. Do you know this meaning?"

"Every eye shall see," cried the heavenly host.

"From ancient times men and angels have heard of this hour," called Gabriel. "Now let them see!"

> *Though he leads*
> *angels,*
> *he is a man.*
> *On him*
> *still*
> *the mark of the Carpenter.*

The only begotten Son of God
about to receive his family,
brothers and sisters
of his species,
the sons and daughters of God
like unto their elder brother.

The Lord, silhouetted in the Door, turned and faced the heavenly armada. Rapture swept the host.

"It is the time of the revealing of the holy ones," announced the Lord. "The end of mortality for the redeemed."

Corruption ends.
Redemption
included naught for
the bodies of the saved.
Now shall the
spirits of the righteous ones
who have been
made holy
receive
their transfigured state.
Their spirits
made alive
and
joined to my life,
their souls restored,
their flesh crucified and destroyed,
each now to receive

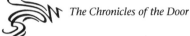

a new body
of heavenly design.
Thus completes
so great a salvation!

The heavenly throng took up the chorus:

So great a salvation!
Salvation to the uttermost!

The Lord looked back over his shoulder and exclaimed,

Gabriel!

The angelic host, knowing Gabriel's part, responded in uncontrolled jubilation. Gabriel raised his mighty trumpet toward his mouth.

With his Lord and one hundred million angels watching, Gabriel steadied his trumpet. The host of angels moved toward the Door. A magnificent moment of silence reigned. Then the Lord turned to face the bright blue ball.

The Carpenter-Creator stepped just outside the Door, then cried one word.

NOW!

CHAPTER
Eleven

In that instant the Carpenter exploded into glory so pure that the eyes of angels were momentarily blinded. In that electric moment Jesus Christ thundered the long-awaited command.

"Descend!

"Now does the Son of Man return in his glory!"

One man and one hundred million angels plunged earthward. As they did, the Lord raised his hands above his head and released the loudest shout that ever would be heard. Nonetheless, that shattering call was accompanied by a resounding trumpet blast which almost matched the Lord's cry both in power and beauty.

As the shout of the Lord and the sound of the trumpet thundered across the galaxies, heaven quaked, and the portal itself shuddered in convulsions, while the bright blue ball trembled in its weary orbit.

In the midst of this most astounding moment, the angels burst forth in accolades to a Lord who was now wrapped in swarming torrents of light.

Though it was but one word that had poured forth from the Lord's mouth, its might penetrated the earth with a power greater than that which he had unleashed when he spoke creation into being. That one awesome word flung itself across two creations and wafted its way to the bright blue ball, there to be heard by all men, those alive and even those who were not.

That one word, now reverberating in every ear, was

ARISE!

Every eye opened; every head lifted toward the skies.

It was a call to the dead and dying, to the known and the forgotten . . . to come forth.

That one word baptized the earth in the power of God. Accompanying that baptism, the blast of Gabriel's trumpet. The entire planet shook under the dueted sounds, calling the dead in Christ to come forth, and the living redeemed to ascend into the skies.

The response to voice and trumpet was instant.

Earth cried out with creaks, groans, and then mighty eruptions. Like myriads of volcanoes bursting up from out of the bowels of the earth, graves began splintering open. Earth, water, and ice exploded and then gave up their captives.

The angels, watching the surface of the earth rupture and ignite, joined in with the sound of Gabriel's trumpet and the Lord's life-giving shout with their own peals of joy. Even earth, it seemed, joined the crescendo as it heaved up the dead to life.

As mortals, ripping open earth's bowels, put on immortality, angels suddenly realized the entire angelic host had become visible to the human eye. Holding to only a semblance of order, they began to cry, "Earth, look up! Earth, receive your Lord. Mankind, behold your Lord!"

And what a sight it was that met the eyes of mankind!

Gabriel had taken up a place just to the side of his Lord, his trumpet continuing its unabated call. On the other side of the Lord was the fiery archangel of vengeance, Michael, his gleaming sword spewing fire, his voice daring the inhabitants of creation to interfere with the Lord's return.

Behind this trio of descending light came a living garland of innumerable angels, their train of blazing light reaching from heaven's Door, then circling downward toward the earth. Full throated, they continued their descent, shouting their praises to a returning Lord.

On they hurtled, led by him who was soon to be known by all as the undisputed Lord of heaven *and* earth.

A startled mankind watched this pageantry of living fire paint itself across the skies in heavenly artistry.

But a scene of equal splendor was unfolding below.

Out of the tombs, out of the oceans, seas, and lakes, out of the frozen north and the frozen south, from deserts, mountains, and wastelands, in the midst of rampages of flying dirt, exploding waters, and cracking ice, former inhabitants of earth, shining like flaming crystal, began rising into the sky.

In a moment the entire surface of the earth was lit with golden fires as men and women, loosed from their graves, took upon themselves their blazing new bodies, blanketing the entire earth with their light.

Eyes of angels, though accustomed to the sight of immutable splendors, blinked in wonder as they watched the earth's mantle gleam with new grandeur. From heaven's view, earth seemed to be suddenly covered with bursting geysers flashing infinite hues of whitest light and brazen fire, all roaring forth into the air.

"It is the holy ones!" cried the host in unison. "The saints enrobed in light. They lift off the earth and mount the skies!"

"Those who are alive in Christ have joined those who were asleep in Christ," shouted Recorder.

The angels cheered.

"Both those dead in Christ and those alive in Christ are laying off mortality. At last, they receive their new and glorious bodies!"

"I did not know their bodies would be *that* glorious," murmured the angel Gloir. "Flesh has changed to glory; the hope of earth is now reality."

Men and women, stunned by their own magnifi-

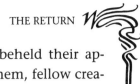

cent change, looked upward and beheld their approaching Lord, while all around them, fellow creatures of salvation rose from the earth, emitting light that would match an archangel.

Clothed in the brightness of the righteousness of God, the holy ones spiraled together into the sky like millions of fiery comets. All eyes of earth and heaven turned nowhere but to Jesus.

Ten thousand times ten thousand impassioned angels whirled their swords above their heads in ecstasy, shouting:

> *"The holy ones!*
> *Earth's surface blazes*
> *with the resurrection bodies*
> *of the holy ones.*
> *They have upon them a glory*
> *until now*
> *reserved only for their Lord,*
> *their bodies now akin to that of his."*

In remembrance of this ecstatic moment, Recorder inscribed the following into the Book of Records.

For one unforgettable, indescribable moment, earth, enveloped in a sight like unto living gold and light, was covered in its former unfallen beauty.

But earth's glory was only for a moment. As the redeemed moved higher into the air, the awesome pageantry of the ascending host swiftly passed from the earth and filled the air, leaving the lonely planet in its fallen state. Now it was the skies that were filled with the flaming splendor of redeemed men and women streaming upward.

The angelic host, not quite holding its ranks, were crying, shouting, praising, and singing.

> *They ascend to meet him,*
> *a multitude without number,*
> *washed in the blood of the Lamb.*
> *The skies have become*
> *a shimmering storm*
> *of glistening gold.*
> *They rise,*
> *shining bodies*
> *clothed in the purity of God.*
> *And he in full descent*
> *and similar array*
> *soon to rendezvous*
> *with his kin.*

"Some of them have looks of amazement on their faces. Some even seem astounded," observed a bemused Rathel.

"Methinks there are many who are quite surprised to find themselves numbered among the elect," chuckled Adorae.

"A good number, indeed," laughed Gloir. "But only for a moment. Look at them."

The wondering eyes of the redeemed had riveted upon one immutable sight—the face of their Lord.

"They have, at last, laid aside their differences," sighed Recorder.

"Forever!" resounded Michael.

At that moment, the redeemed found their new voices. Issuing from their throats came a living cataract of praise.

In response to their adulation, the splendor that was Christ radiated out to touch the glory of the redeemed swarming ever closer to him.

From the lips of the Carpenter came the exhilarated cry,

Come!

The shouts of angels half out of their spirits, the wild cries of joy bursting from the lungs of airborne earthlings flooding into the skies, joined by Gabriel's trumpet, all mingled together to bless creation with the grandest choir that an envying earth would ever hear.

At that moment Michael, peering deeply into the midst of the ascending saints, caught sight of an old friend.

CHAPTER
Twelve

"Look!" exclaimed Michael, "I see Adam, there, among the ascending ones."

"Look at Adam!" shouted the entire angelic host in unison.

The eyes of heaven had turned their piercing eyes on an old friend from ages past. What met their eyes unleashed from their ranks one mighty, uproarious cheer.

"It is back, it is back! Adam has his *light* back! He is once more robed in light."

"Oh, joy of heaven's desire," wept Exalta. "At last we see Red Earth in his intended state."

"Adam! Oh, Adam! I watched your light go out and disappear," roared the angel Adorae, half crying, half shouting.

"Look at him now. He once more *glows!* The clothing of light, lost in the Garden of Eden, restored!"

"More magnificent than before," exuded Exalta.

"Adam, your new body, *more* than innocent! More than pure! A body clothed in God's own righteousness."

"Robed in a glory surpassing even the highest angels," mumbled an awestruck Gabriel.

The first of the race of men, his arms raised above his head, called upward to his angelic friends in that inimitable voice which they so well remembered but which had so long been unheard.

> *By the blood of the Lamb*
> *now are the sons*
> *and daughters*
> *of men made perfect.*
> *And by his life*
> *we are added*
> *to his own.*

It was at that moment that stunned angels, gasping in awe, caught sight of Eve. It took incredible beauty to hush angels in such a moment, yet Eve's startling reappearance had done just that.

> *More beautiful than before.*
> *More beautiful*
> *than heaven's*
> *highest lore.*

"What can this mean?" whispered Michael reverently, when at last he found his voice.

Recorder, remembering the enigma still hidden in Eve, grew pensive in his musings.

"Adam, in the garden, a picture of Christ. Adam, a

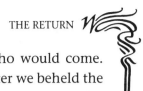

foreshadowing of the true Man who would come. Our eyes saw Adam, the picture. Later we beheld the reality, even Christ.

"Eve, like Adam, you are also a foreshadowing. You also foretell of someone who is to come. Today I see you, Eve. But I do not yet see the reality! Where, Eve, is the woman you foreshadow?"

Recorder turned to Michael and, for the very first time, sought insight from another.

"Michael, how can there be anything more beautiful, more glorious than the Eve we now behold? And if a woman is to exist who is the reality of what Eve foreshadows, *where* is that woman? Where is that woman who surpasses Eve in glory?

Where are you,
woman beyond all womanhood?
Where are you,
counterpart of Christ?
Where are you,
whom Eve
does but announce?

"You are beautiful beyond all, Eve. In every move and in every word you tell us of one who is still hidden from our eyes. But *where* is that girl? Where is she who is that ultimate purpose of God?

"Somewhere, someday, the woman you represent . . . awaits. *That* will be the hour of *final revealings!* That woman will show us beauty and glory as far beyond Eve as the glory of Christ is beyond that of Adam."

Realizing that two great multitudes were about to converge, Michael tore himself from the moment. He lifted his voice above the din of praise and shouted a command to the angels.

CHAPTER
Thirteen

"Fall back, O angels of God. Make room for the redeemed."

Transfixed angels, beyond themselves as they watched the ascending ones, reluctantly slipped backward to make room for the sons and daughters of God.

The Lord thrust out his arms toward the ascending lights of men, then raised his hands upward in a gesture of invitation. Two throngs, one ascending, one descending, roared their approval.

"What a meeting! What a meeting this is going to be," laughed Recorder.

"Yonder," exclaimed Gabriel. "See who is there, near to the side of Adam."

"It is Abraham," exclaimed Michael. "What a sight. Now there is a thing worthy of disbelief!" roared Michael in delight.

"Listen to him."

Today
I
who was the seed

behold my descendants—
as numerous as the stars.
And he who is
my one descendant—
oh!—
he was the seed
of my seed.
But today
I am seed
of his seed.

"Look again," urged Gabriel. "Moses! But where is his stern demeanor? He is wholly unlike himself. He seems joy itself. And his words, listen to his words."

Grace! Grace! Grace!
Naught of myself
Naught of laws!
Nor fear.
Not one of them
has brought me here.
Grace, grace, grace
this day
has found its name—
that name is Jesus!

"Look at them, all of them. They all are so beautiful. More beautiful than angels in highest splendor," cried an ecstatic Michael.

"How wondrous," replied a whispering Gabriel.

Convulsing with sobs and tears, the two archangels embraced one another in fervent joy.

In other circumstances Recorder might have registered dismay at such unbecoming behavior on the part of Michael and Gabriel. But on this particular occasion the very opposite proved to be true. The ever stoic recording angel swept across the skies and joined his two companions in a trilogy of wild embrace.

"Recorder!" protested Michael. "Your place . . . the books!"

"Have I no rights? Am I so poor that I alone of all the host of heaven and earth am to be denied this moment? Besides, the Book of Records is almost full. Much less than a page is all that remains."

Michael laughed as he beheld in Recorder's face something none would have thought possible. But it was Gabriel who spoke the words.

"Recorder! Your face. You weep!"

"I have reason," replied a sobbing Recorder. *"They are all here!!"*

> *On the day the Lord created me*
> *my Lord handed to me*
> *the Book of Life.*
> *The book was full*
> *of names*
> *And all were recorded*
> *in my handwriting*
> *though I had never*
> *written!*

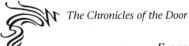

From that hour
I have feared:
that some name therein listed
might not be here
upon this holy day.
But
they are all present.
Not one is missing!
Every name
written in
the Book of Life.
Oh, amazing grace,
They are all here!

Michael would not have answered Recorder if he could have, for the glory of that moment banished words.

Gabriel, drowning in the delirium of joy, declared, "Let us behold that moment when the holy ones arrive in his presence."

With those words Gabriel soared into the midst of the angels, took his place in the very center, and awaited the arrival of the resurrected ones.

CHAPTER
Fourteen

"They are more beautiful than we," whispered Gloir blissfully as he watched the space between the Lord and the redeemed narrowing.

"They are of greater majesty and splendor than all else that dwells in creation, save God alone."

"As it should be. As it should be," responded Adorae, in what might be described as a heave of solemn relief.

"They are beautiful beyond beauty," agreed Gloir. "And pure!"

"I do believe they can outshout us. I have never heard anything like it. Nor have any of us," observed a charmed Adorae, listening intently to the praises of the holy ones as they drew ever closer.

"Seraphim would fold their wings," added a spellbound Exalta.

"And cherubim lose their fury!" agreed Rathel.

"They can see us, can they not?" wondered Exalta aloud.

"Your question should be, even if they can, do they care!" responded Adorae. "Their eyes are only on him. I am not sure that they ever will pay us much mind, as long as there stands in their midst the transcendent presence of our Lord."

"Listen to them! They have somehow all found one voice. They have joined in one shout! Listen! They have found one song which all are singing. They have the *instincts* of heaven!" gasped Rathel.

Even as Rathel spoke, the angelic host realized they, too, knew this joyous new song and could, therefore, join in the singing. The very thought of such a blended choir sent the angels into ecstasy.

From every throat of the redeemed of mankind rose one grand song of praise, lifted in adoration to their Lord. Eyes brightened as they heard angels above, for the first time ever, add their voices in song with man's. As the anthem neared its rousing end, the rapturous voice of the Lord joined in.

It was simply too much for any to contain.

The song of praise ended with the thunderous roar of jubilant angels, the redeemed matching them in volume and melody.

The messengers of God, as by some mysterious signal, burst into dazzling splendor never before known to them. Like a string of blazing meteors, they formed a vast circle above their Lord, creating a canopy of swirling light.

The golden light of life flowing forth from within the redeemed spewed forth a kaleidoscope of luminance that reached out and touched the descending angels. The majestic radiance of angels, aflame with joy, beamed across the redeemed. And in the midst, Jesus Christ, caught in the cross fire of glory.

It was at that particular moment the redeemed broke through the clouds above the earth. Myriads of translated human beings swept into space, shouting greetings to their Lord!

For the first time in the annals of angels, not one face was dry. For the first time in the annals of mankind, not one face bore tears.

The Lord halted his descent.

"He awaits their arrival."

Citizens of the heavenlies enlarged their circle and waited.

The inhabitants of realms alien to each other were about to become kin.

At last the redeemed reached the Lord. Pure and perfect sons and daughters of God surrounded their Lord in a vast circle, the light of their perfection forming a ring of blazing fire around him.

Having fully encircled their Lord, the holy ones broke out in cries of triumph. As they did angels, beyond any hope of discipline, broke ranks and poured down into the midst of the redeemed. Joyful shouts of men set free from the fall blended with cries of joy coming from transported angels.

Two realms now one formed the grandest gathering creation would ever record.

Shouts thundered above shouts. Glory mingled with glory.

Men and angels embraced, then cried out with

shouts not unlike the shout of victory rising from their Lord. Glorious bedlam reigned as glorious bedlam should when men and angels meet in the skies. The holy ones of God and the messengers of God at last found common ground as all fell upon their faces, giving worship to him to whom all worship is due.

CHAPTER
Fifteen

"It was the greatest gathering that ever has been," sighed Michael.

"Agreed," replied the recording angel.

"Or ever will be," added Michael. "Eternity's crowning hour."

"Not so," came Recorder's surprising answer.

"What!" exclaimed a startled Michael. "A yet grander hour than this?" he stammered incredulously. "What could it be! There is no grander hour than his ingathering . . . is there?"

In a voice of unnerving evenness, Recorder repeated his words: "There *will* be a grander hour." He paused and added, "Perhaps *two* grander hours!"

"Can you speak of them?" probed Michael.

"The hour when this creation, the heavens and the earth, *dissolve*. When the entire creation, even the favored planet, vanishes. Forever. And then, the appearance of the new heavens and the new earth. Redeemed mankind is a new creation, even a new biological species. This new species must have its own environs. Yes, a new heaven and earth. But more, a new habitat for the holy ones."

"Oh!" was Michael's embarrassed response.

After a pause, Michael edged out another question. "Did you not say there might possibly be *two* grander hours?"

"The highest moment, the grandest of all hours, will come at the full revelation and the complete revealing of *the Mystery*."

Quiet astonishment was Michael's only response.

"The Mystery, becoming a living, breathing reality," choked a trembling Recorder.

"When . . . when will that be?!"

"Oh no! Not you, too," rumbled Recorder. "You angels! You are just like men! You always want to know *when*. How should I know? Am I the advisor of God? He seeks the counsel of no man and no angel. Angels do not know and—contrary to human guesswork—man does not know. God knows, and we guess. I might add that our guesses seem always to be in error."

"You have no idea?"

"None," grumbled Recorder again. "For all I know, perhaps *today* . . . as men count time. Or tomorrow. Or, perhaps, a thousand years from now. I do not know. And you would be wise to join me in my ignorance and go about keeping the charge given you."

Michael blinked. For a moment he was not quite sure how an archangel was to respond to so bold a word.

"But that day *will* arrive, Recorder?"

"It will!" came a most emphatic reply.

"Then I shall wait and see."

"Perhaps you thought you had some other choice in the matter?" sighed Recorder.

"I suppose not," replied the subdued archangel.

The Lord Jesus
had at last
descended from
out of the heavenlies
with a cry of
command,
with the voice of
an archangel,
and
with the trumpet of God.
The dead in Christ
did
rise first.
Then,
those who were alive
were caught up
and,
rising into the clouds,
they met him
in the air.
And they shall be with
the Lord
forever.

PART

IV

CHAPTER
Sixteen

Such a groaning had never been heard. Earth was in travail, its moans reverberating across the galaxy.

Earth was in prayer, a prayer provoked by jealousy, for earth had witnessed the liberation of the redeemed from their mortal bondage. Now the fallen planet begged for a similar deliverance. Had redemption or, failing that, annihilation ever been so plaintively requested? Or doom implored? A tired and dying earth, creaking in its ruptured orbit, wept in the presence of the shame of its continued existence.

Heaven, hearing the earthen prayer, joined in with its own petition for annihilation. Each called to the other with quakes and tremors, bemoaning the loss of their former glorious estate. Humiliation grew unbearable as they witnessed man so utterly delivered from so equal a fall and translated into so grand an estate.

The echoes of their pain filled the spheres.

Mercy answered.

Earth's bowels began to rip open. Heaven's vaults crumbled. Earth and stars, moon and sky, heaven's floor and heaven's roof sounded their death rattle. Demons and fallen angels, seeing their habitat above the earth in seizures, fled in terror.

"Michael, your sword, lend it to me," spoke a voice from behind.

"No one takes Michael's sword," rebuffed the archangel as he turned to face such impertinence.

"Recorder! You! You would wield a sword . . . even *my* sword!?"

"The time for earth's salvation has come. Yes, I will wield *that* sword; give it to me," responded the only created voice Michael might obey.

"You spoke of another glorious hour. I perceive that hour is upon us? Has that *time* arrived?"

"No, Michael. Time *ends!*"

With that, Michael relinquished his sword to the most trustable of all angels. Every angel—elect and damned—turned fascinated eyes toward Recorder as he bolted across the skies; nor were they at all surprised that the most ancient of angels wielded that imposing sword with unnerving ease.

Three archangels and three angelic armies stood like statues as Recorder took up a place midway between earth and heaven.

"What foolish thing is this?" hissed a contemptuous Lucifer.

Planting both feet firmly in the vacant sky, Recorder lifted the sword of wrath above his head, then turned, first toward earth, and then toward heaven.

To the astonishment of all, heaven and earth be-

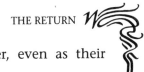

gan to move toward one another, even as their agonizing cries ended.

> *Cease now your strife*
> *O Time.*
> *Eternity at last*
> *has won!*

> *I swear*
> *by the holiness of*
> *God:*
> *The pages*
> *of the Book of Records*
> *are full.*
> *One last entry remains*
> *to be written,*
> *awaiting its*
> *space*
> *to record*
> *the death of time.*

> *Space, find your end.*
> *Matter, be vanquished.*
> *Frail time, be no more.*
> *This is your last hour.*
> *Now marks the end*
> *of marking.*

> *Hear me,*
> *dreary heaven*

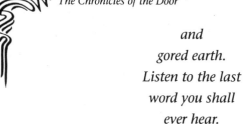

*and
gored earth.
Listen to the last
word you shall
ever hear.*

*I, Recorder,
watched you in your birth
and recorded your
every hour.
You, creation,
so firmly set
yet so
temporally made:
Be gone!*

*He who made
this worn and ancient creation
now brings that creation back again
to its first state.
Creation,
hear me:
Your Creator
returns you now to
nothingness.*

With those words uttered, earth screamed as had never anything screamed before, then burst into molten fire. From within the inferno there rose one last praise, then a final burst of heat and fire. Earth vanished.

"Thank God. Thank our Lord," rose the voices of elect men and angels.

Earth is delivered
from her pain,
no more to live in shame,
no more to wax and wane.

Recorder solemnly turned and pointed the burning sword toward the vast realm of the invisible.

All that is not of God,
all that is not divine,
take your leave of eternity.
All glories save the
throne of God
and the garden
yield up your space.
Make room for greater glory.
Heavens old
now vanish
and make place for
heaven new.

Galaxies collapsed and fell in on one another; skies and stars followed hard on. The invisible heavens rent, the wall that had been the Boundary, the sapphire floor, all crumbled, shattered, and then exploded into flames.

Angels watched in silence as their home devoured itself in a fiery holocaust.

Amid the hungry flames there rose from heaven's heart an ode of thanksgiving for so grand a deliverance.

The heavens—seen and unseen—became *oblivion*, while silent angels stared into an endless gorge of nothingness.

With a strength that gave pause to every angel, Recorder effortlessly hurled the sword back to Michael. The strong hand of Michael caught the flaming weapon, lifted it high above his head, and raised a spirit-chilling cry of defiance.

Not fully understanding Michael's warring stance, elect angels grabbed for their swords, then turned about, for Recorder was speaking again.

Behold,
one last act unplayed.
When done,
then ends
all that is old!
To be
forgotten
forever,
not even in dreams
to be recalled.

Behold the last scene,

and
when fulfilled
I render up the golden pen,
never
to write again.
For no more
are there times
or
worlds
to chronicle.

One last sentence
then ends my charge.
Then am I free
to praise my Lord
throughout the new
eternity.

Now do I write
my final verse.
Hear me demons:
'tis
to record
the end
of all
that is
perverse.

Hard upon those words there came the strangest
sound, and a shaking stranger still.

"It is the *non*," whispered Michael.

"There is no such place," responded the hushed voice of Gabriel.

"Now there is!" replied Michael. "Look for yourself. At last. *The Pit!!*"

In the midst of an oblivion now wholly void of the former creation, there emerged a darkness beyond dark, belching flames darker still.

"Its depths, unfindable! Its end, as broad as eternity," pondered Gabriel.

Eerie whirls of black fires and sulfuric fumes gurgled their invitation to all that remained that was unredeemed.

"The Pit! At last, the Pit," repeated the intrepid Michael.

In a voice so hushed no ears but Michael's could hear, Recorder whispered. "Old comrade, you have waited long for this moment. Unleash your rapier of wrath, take full vengeance now, O avenging angel. Now, Michael. With all your spirit . . . *Now!*"

As the last word fell from Recorder's lips, Michael, set free from all restraint, released a bellicose roar that rumbled across the chasm and made its way to the ears of the infernal ones.

To the finale of the fall.

Then, with eyes exploding fire, Michael whipped his menacing sword above his head, whirling it

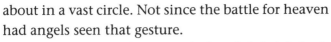

about in a vast circle. Not since the battle for heaven had angels seen that gesture.

"I have seen that fury once before." Gabriel shuddered. "That is the rage we all beheld when Michael led the elect ones in so violent an assault it drove the fallen angels out of heaven and into the skies above the earth."

The blur that was Michael suddenly stopped, his sword now pointing in but one direction, that place where only a few moments earlier had been the planet earth.

In words ringing with command and defiance, Michael yielded up a war cry.

"Come to me, O perditious one!"

An ecstatic host of elect angels unsheathed their weapons and, with Michael, charged toward the host of the damned even as Michael bellowed:

The final battle!

CHAPTER
Seventeen

The warriors of God paired off, one from the ranks of Gabriel with one from those of Michael's charge, then hurled themselves toward the empty skies where once had hung the bright blue ball.

The voice of a raging Michael sounded again and again, its sole intent to curdle the spirits of demons. "Drive them to the pit," he commanded. "But let none touch Lucifer, for he is mine and mine alone."

The ranks of the terrified rebels, now devoid of their habitat above a vanished earth, dissolved in disarray. Some dropped their swords, others slashed aimlessly at the air, while others, in total panic, sought an avenue of escape from their encircling foes.

Nowhere did the battle belong to any except the forces of life. Like a tidal wave of living fire they flamed forward unrelentingly, forcing their despised enemies toward a belching pit. In a moment swift beyond belief, the retreating forces of darkness found themselves standing precariously at the edge of the lusting chasm.

"You will say it! Say it and say it now," demanded the angels of God.

The routed forces of evil, surrounded on every side, their faces gaunt with fear and their minds twisted by horror, screeched their discordant reply, "Never! Never shall we say it!"

"You *will* say it. And you will say it *now!*"

"Though our bowels burn forever in the abyss, never will we say it."

As the protestations of the infernal ones rose in yet wilder vows of refusal, someone familiar to *all* the angelic host suddenly appeared. The din of noise abated.

"Red Earth!" cried the rebels gleefully in their remembrance of their past exploits.

Adorned in a robe of purest white, *Adam* strode into the midst of the chaotic scene.

"You will own him to be the Son of God?" queried Adam.

"Yes," roared the fallen angels, "but no other."

"You *will* confess him to be the Son of Man."

"Never," they screeched. "Man is below us. You, Adam, are our proof that we defeated man . . . man whom God sent to rule earth."

"Then God did not come in the flesh?" questioned Adam in a voice not quite a taunt.

"Never!!" they cried again.

"I suppose you do not recall that it was a *man* who was to be lord of earth?"

In yelps of delight the dark angels replied, "Yes.

Yes, but we fouled the plan of God. We stopped *you*,
Red Earth! You never became ruler of earth. You
became a slave to sin. Death entered by you; and in
so dire a course *you* became our fairest trophy. Earth
was not ruled by man! Remember, Adam, that slaves,
not rulers, were your sons!"

Their ridicules became jeers, and jeers turned into
a piercing chant. "We brought down the race of
Adam!" But the noise waned as the damned ones
began to realize that Adam showed no shame at the
reproachful reminder of his catastrophic failure.

"There were *two* men," responded Adam in a voice
both cool, quiet, and devastatingly confident.

Indistinct whines and whimpers met his words.
Adam crossed his arms and looked defiantly into the
faces of his former masters. After an electrifying
moment, he spoke again.

"The sons of Adam all failed, as did I, their father.
But there was *another* man."

The damned froze in word and movement.

"*That man* . . . you did not bring down *that* man!"
continued Adam solemnly.

"Defeat was *yours,* not his. *That* one shall rule the
earth. God's purpose for man, to rule earth, *is* fulfilled!"

Adam smiled, his calm and strength unnerving
even Michael.

"*You* failed," repeated the emboldened Adam. "Sin
is vanquished. The son of sin, even Death, is *dead."*

Adam paused, threw up his hands, and declared in

grand finality, "The race of Adam is no more. It is extinct, and it has been ever since the cross. A new race, a new species of man has emerged," he cried in triumph.

Again Adam stared into the faces of the citizens of a kingdom to which he had once belonged. Then he trumpeted: "Do you not realize, O sons of awaiting damnation, even Adam no longer belongs to Adam's fallen race! I am delivered out of that race. I am delivered out of *your* kingdom. I now belong to, and am one of, a biologically new species. I am, as are all these others, of the line of a new man. We are descendents of a new race of whom Jesus Christ is head!"

A groan of dark realization swept across the rebellious ones.

"I have been brought into a new creation and have become one among a new species of mankind destined for a new creation. I, Adam, belong not to Adam's race.

"Damned, demonic forces, look at me. Do I look fallen? Know, here at your end, you *failed* because that second man destroyed my species upon a cursed tree. *That* man you never defeated. You have failed. It is he, not you, who vanquished my race. He vanquished me upon the destroying tree. Then did he ransom me out of my race and your kingdom into a new kingdom and into a new, *triumphant* race."

Because this grand confessional came from no less than the mouth of Adam and was delivered with such unbridled boldness, the derision of the damned turned to fevered delirium. The forces of evil—whose sole purpose had been to defeat and enslave the third highest form of life and bring it into the dark kingdom of the second highest life—now had to look into the face of that very man and realize he was no longer part of the third highest life, nor even the second highest life. They were looking at one named Adam who was now a member of the highest life.

Dark realization bore deeper into the doomed spirits of doomed angels.

"Red Earth *has* eaten of the fruit of the Tree of Life," they screeched in horror.

"See now, damned ones, a still greater horror," announced an Adam who had divine life in him.

The fallen angels looked above them. Encircling the angels of darkness were no less than the holy ones—even the redeemed!

"Your judges!" invoked Gabriel, the fist of his right hand lifted above his head.

"Face now the ultimate indignation," rumbled Rathel.

Not one among the redeemed spoke, for a verdict was not necessary. The absolute holiness, the utter righteousness, the perfect purity of the ransomed ones was of itself the final pronouncement of condemnation upon the citizens of doom.

The eyes of the damned sought not to see.

"Look upon us," commanded Adam.

"Robed in the whitest of garments—pure, spotless, *saved* . . . saved to the uttermost—the life of God in one and all. Look at us, you sons of the pit."

From the lips of every child of God roared the grand confessional, holy to men, blasphemous to fallen angels.

"God came in the flesh. God came as man.

"You will say it," came their commanding roar.

Unable to restrain their joy at the sight of so bold a remonstration, the heavenly host joined in the grand confessional, even as the damned clawed at their ears.

As final confrontation and ultimate judgment approached, the Lord Jesus appeared.

"Son of God," screamed the demons.

"Yes," thundered the believers, *"and* Son of Man."

The citizens of darkness were about to protest again but stopped short. The light of the glory of the Lord began to flow forth *unrestrained.* The damned became blinded in the presence of such astounding glory. Even the elect angels were forced to shield their eyes, but not before they noted that the sons and daughters of God, unblinking, did but absorb and then reflect the Lord's enraptured state.

Counterwise, the demonic host began to go insane, for the light of his glory, joined with that of the holy ones, was destroying the mind of their spirits. Screaming, cursing, flinging damnations, and gnashing their teeth, the legion of the damned went

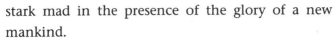

stark mad in the presence of the glory of a new mankind.

Gradually the light of the Lord's glory began to recede.

"The Lord is enfolding his resplendency," whispered Recorder, finding his sight in lessened glory.

What met the eyes of angels as they recovered their sight was a Lord whose eyes blazed like burning brass and whose face shined as a thousand suns. But still his glory continued to enfold. At last glory vanished. There stood before the angels a very ordinary looking man.

"The Carpenter!" choked Exalta, his face drenched with tears. "The Carpenter," he whispered again, as he fell to his knees. The redeemed, too, dropped to their knees.

Before the believers and before both elect and damned angels stood the most ordinary appearing of men, wearing the simple garb of a Nazarene laborer.

Damned angels, convulsing in madness, discovered that blinding glory had whelmed them to their knees.

"The Nazarene! No! Take from us the sight of this one," they begged.

Driven beyond madness by this intolerable sight, the damned continued screaming.

"Leave us, Son of Man!" pleaded the tortured spirits. That confession, delivered in delirium, became a discordant chant offered up in madness. With those

95

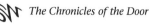

words dropping from their lips, the messengers of wickedness at last raised their declaration:

> *God came in the flesh.*
> *Jesus Christ is Lord.*
> *A man,*
> *a carpenter from Nazareth,*
> *even*
> *Jesus,*
> *is Lord!*
> *Jesus Christ is Lord!*

Angels of God, their swords turned to molten fire, rose up to drive the condemned toward the yawning pit, crying as they came, "Meet now your sure destruction."

The pit, seeming to come alive, issued a greeting of belching fire and smoke to the damned. In fits of rage and vows of defiance the messengers of Satan stumbled into their final abode.

As the last of those wicked ones plunged into the lake of fire, every eye turned toward Michael and Lucifer.

CHAPTER
Eighteen

"You are free from all constraints of time, Michael."

It was the voice of the Lord. "You are free to reveal to your enemy that which your eyes and the eyes of Recorder witnessed on the day I was crucified."

"Show me what you will, Galilean," interrupted a defiant Lucifer. "I shall never bow my knee to you."

Angered at such insolence, Michael stepped in front of the fallen archangel. "Look now at what is behind you."

Lucifer turned. Behind him lay a vast opening, its purpose and content unknown to Lucifer.

"Against your wildest protestations and strongest resistance you shall be driven through that portal. What you will see are things which were shown to me long ago. I visited places which are not places, and witnessed mysteries beyond men and angels."

"What is that to me?" retorted Lucifer.

Biting every word, Michael replied. "I saw *this very hour.* I have seen *this* very battle which you and I are about to engage in. *Now,* Lucifer, you shall also see. And having seen, you *shall bow!!"*

Recorder, who had long ago been a witness to this same moment, was somehow managing to both laugh and cry.

For the last time, the two most powerful archangels drew their weapons and crossed the two most awesome swords ever known.

"Final combat, Lucifer," whispered Michael, his face radiating both rage and glee.

Michael whirled about in full circle. Lucifer swiftly raised his sword. The two swords clashed together, Lucifer meeting Michael's strength with equal strength.

"Can this battle ever be concluded? Shall it not last forever?" wondered Gabriel.

Michael whirled again. The speed and might were too great for Lucifer's sword. He stepped back.

Again, with a swiftness even angels' eyes could not follow, Michael whirled full circle again. Once more Lucifer retreated.

"Michael is forcing him into the portal. What lies within? Events of the past? Even though Michael has declared they are events which no eye has ever seen?" wondered Gabriel.

"Yes, Gabriel, the past. Yet things no eyes have ever seen!" affirmed Recorder.

The air was filled with Lucifer's curses and Michael's vows of vengeance. It was a battle between pride and wrath, Lucifer's vestment flashing beautiful hues of blue and red, while Michael's flooded forth gold and white.

Though his taunts never abated, Lucifer was forced
to give ground to the fierceness of Michael's rage.

"Drive me across the firmament, across eternity,
yet never can you harm me. Never will I surrender."

Michael's arm came down on Lucifer's sword with
a force that surprised even Michael. Lucifer, following his beleaguered sword, stumbled. Michael lowered his sword and stepped back.

"No?" responded Michael coolly. "Best then you
turn and see where it is you have been driven."

The angel of light cautiously turned his head,
peered into the eerie surroundings, and swore at the
scene which lay just behind him.

"We are passing back through time! To Golgotha!
You would drive me back to the day your God died?!
Of what use is such foolishness?"

"You will see as never you have seen, foul foe. And
in seeing, find the fool you are. Now to your guard."

The sword of Michael, driven by ascending rage,
moved again with blinding speed, delivering blows
beyond any the Prince of Darkness had ever tasted.

Stumbling, rising, and then stumbling again, Satan found his only security in backward flight. Out
of the corner of his eyes he discerned that he stood
at the foot of the cross. Then, pushed beyond the
cross, Lucifer came into full view of Golgotha, of the
cross, and of the dying Carpenter.

Michael lowered his sword.

"You have been allowed here, as once I was.

Behold that which ne'er you dreamed. Find, now, what truly transpired upon this bloody knoll."

Death appeared.

Lucifer listened intently as he watched a bargain struck by Jesus and Death. Knowing full well that he could neither be seen nor heard, he nonetheless cried in fiendish delight at the sight of Sin's accumulation at the cross, jeered at the dying of the Son of God, and frothed with glee as the Carpenter became sin.

But glee turned to terror as he realized Death was being driven, unwillingly, into the bosom of the Galilean.

"Not so!" cried Lucifer. "We fiendish friends have often cavorted together since that day!"

"There has been no 'since that day' in the chronicles of God," remonstrated Michael. "Now look full on."

The world's entire system, a fallen cosmos, slipped into the breast of the Crucified One, followed hard on by the entire race of Adam's lineage. Lucifer watched in awe as the flesh of fallen man was nailed to the cross. When this race ended, so also ended all rules, ordinances, and rituals . . . even the law, the Sabbath, religious observances, festivals, and seasons! Then, into the bosom of the Carpenter disappeared even the governments of this world.

"Now learn of God, foul foe," snarled Michael as he motioned to his enemy to look again.

The father of unbelief stared in disbelief as he

watched his own self, wholly disarmed, being thrust into the body of the dying Savior. Before he could raise his voice in protest, he saw *his* kingdom, the very kingdom of darkness, plunged into the Son of Man.

Lucifer screamed in repulsion, "None of these things happened!"

With eyes spewing black fire, he screamed again as he watched his whole realm of rule and power disappear into Jesus, a sound of madness now discernible in his screams.

Suddenly Lucifer's blasphemous declinations ended.

"What is this event I now see taking place upon the cross, so long ago? Impossible! For I saw this same thing happen only a moment ago!"

Lucifer watched in fascination as earth and heaven vanished inside the corpse hanging on the cursed tree.

"Twice? It is not possible," he sputtered.

"Once, long past, at Calvary, and then . . . again . . . only a moment ago . . . heaven and earth destroyed? I watched heaven and earth consumed in fire. Did it happen *twice?*" muttered a confused Lucifer.

"Nay, old serpent. All things are inside God. He sees all time at once. History's whole journey is in him. For him, all things are *the now!* The Lord, who is outside of and sovereign over time, sees all things in the present; and where time is not, all things *are* the present.

"You have seen little here, Lucifer. And learned

less. Now discover what you can neither believe nor understand. I ask you. *When do you think these things happened?"*

"At Golgotha. At Jerusalem. Long ago. But I did not see such things, nor do I believe these events ever transpired," retaliated the prince of principalities.

"No, fiend! You err on both your suppositions," boomed Michael. "You have beheld events which took place in time. As I have learned, so learn you: Time and space are unsure places to see things. *Now see these same events in their full reality!* Watch them unfold, not in time, but in the eternals."

Lucifer's eyes began to whip back and forth as he tried to grasp Michael's meaning. Refusing to either see or believe, he rammed his fists over his eyes.

Michael lunged forward and ripped at Lucifer's hands.

"You will look full on."

The view of Golgotha was growing indistinct. Not disappearing, but *changing;* moving from earth's time and shadows to eternity's reality.

The Carpenter, no longer hanging on a cross, had changed and had become a lamb. A slain lamb.

"When was this?" came Satan's hoarse query.

"Slain when? Slain where? Slain by what forces?" he demanded.

Golgotha's tree, a dead Galilean, events that took place at a stated time, on a stated day, had suddenly become one with events that had taken place in the eternals *at the moment of creation.*

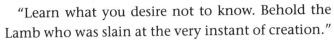

"Learn what you desire not to know. Behold the Lamb who was slain at the very instant of creation."

Lucifer stood mesmerized before an event he knew nothing of.

"It almost looks like Golgotha. Only it is a Lamb. Or is it the Carpenter!?" growled Lucifer. "This happened *before* my own entrance into creation?"

Lucifer watched as an entire creation, *not yet created,* slipped into the slain Lamb.

"Creation is crucified? Taken into death? At the very moment it is being created?" muttered a baffled Lucifer. "Before it was created, creation was crucified? That simply cannot be!"

Once more Lucifer was forced to witness Sin, Death, the law, principalities, all powers, all ordinances and rules, the entire race of the sons and daughters of Adam, the world system, the entire creation . . . *and Lucifer himself,* plunge into the Lamb who was slain *from the foundation of the worlds!*

"I, disarmed? I, plunged into a dying lamb . . . before I was created!" groaned the rebellious one.

"You, disarmed . . . you . . . taken out before you ever began."

"Defeated? I . . . defeated . . . *before* . . ." replied Lucifer in a voice drenched in futility and edging toward derangement.

"Unfair, unfair!" he whined.

Again Lucifer began to tear at his face and gouge at his unbelieving eyes. This time Michael stepped back.

"Defeated?" screeched Lucifer. "My rebellion resolved *before* I rebelled. It cannot be true," he ranted.

Enraged and wholly out of control, Lucifer began to scream and scream again, hoping to scream truth out of his diminishing mind. Soon his screams became trilled yelps and squeals, even as he flailed his arms and beat upon his head, trying desperately to exorcise reality.

In one last instant of sanity, an addled Lucifer looked up at Michael and mumbled piteously, "It is not true! Michael, tell me it is not true!"

Stepping into Lucifer's space, Michael yanked the babbling archangel's sword from his hand.

"You are now disarmed even as you have been disarmed since the cross. Yea, even since creation."

"No. Oh, no. Am I disarmed? Have I ever been?" sputtered the dark archangel.

"Not true, you say, Serpent? Then let me show you something more that your eyes have never seen."

The mighty Michael grabbed Lucifer by the head and forced him to his knees, then pulled back Lucifer's hair, exposing his neck. There, upon the back of Satan's neck, were branded three words.

Crucified Before Created

"Lucifer, you were born . . . *crucified*. So also were all the forces of your domain. And you knew it not!" proclaimed Michael.

Instantly the scene changed.

Michael and his incoherent captive reappeared beside the multitude of elect angels and ransomed men. As one, men and angels encircled them. Again, grabbing Lucifer by the hair of his head, Michael dragged the beleaguered demon into the midst of the angels, past Gabriel, past Recorder, past ten thousand times ten thousand angels, then on through the multitude of the innumerable redeemed. On and on he dragged his senseless foe through the throng so that every eye of all the holy ones might see.

The only sound heard was that of angels' swords being sheathed for the very last time.

"His rebellion ends as it began, in madness," whispered Rathel.

"My foe," cried Michael, "let *your* eyes now look upon the final sight ever they will see. Let them behold the redeemed! Pure, righteous, and unblameable.

"Look upon the holy ones, foul foe!" commanded Michael. "Know that the last vestige of that creation which you caused to fall is gone. Gone, and soon to be forgotten. That creation, and you with it, will be remembered no more. Forever!!"

Lucifer's crazed eyes searched the faces of the redeemed as he passed them, but the only evidence of his recognition was in discordant grunts and whimpers.

"You who were made to be their servant, for a moment you made the chosen ones to be your slaves. But now behold their final state, Lucifer. They stand before you not as your lesser nor your equal. These who stand before you are your judge. More! Now are they the children and family of the Lord. The biological sons and daughters of God!

"Failed! How great your failure, archfiend!"

A cowering Lucifer, looking about wildly, seemed to see nothing.

Angels and men glared at the one remaining citizen of an old and vanished creation while the avenging angel, his vengeance complete, pulled the craven archangel to his last rendezvous. Michael leaned over and whispered into Lucifer's ear, "Now will you say it, ever-defeated foe!"

With those words Michael dragged a stumbling, disbelieving Lucifer to the feet of Jesus.

CHAPTER
Nineteen

For a moment sound did not exist.

Then Michael made a most incredible announcement. "One last word, O damned one. This moment has been given to me *to tell you who you really are!* In so doing, all history comes to its close.

"You now kneel before the *man* who defeated you. Yet you will not own him as Lord. Then in *his* presence learn *who you are.*

"You had but power. He *is* authority. Ever were you subject to his sovereignty. *You are but his servant. Always have you been his servant.* Rebellious one, there was never a moment in all your existence but you were serving the will of God! Hear me, Lucifer: You are, and always have been, a vessel of God."

Lucifer, tearing his hair and beating at his neck, commenced to scream again. In the midst of this demonic fit the fiend fell at last upon his face and cried, "God has come in the flesh."

Jesus Christ is Lord!

And so it came to pass, as had been predicted.

Every knee did bow.
Every tongue
did
confess
that Jesus Christ
is
Lord!

Michael loosed his scabbard and let it fall from his waist.

It was this lot
given to me
to cast you into
that only place
for which you're
fit:
the burning, blazing
pit!

The sinews and muscles of Michael's mighty arms bulged in their strength as he reached down and clutched the Prince of Darkness and lifted the maddened archdemon high above his head.

"I cannot die," screeched Lucifer.

"No. Far worse. You will forever dying be."

Michael moved triumphantly through the throng of the redeemed and then into the midst of the

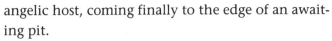

angelic host, coming finally to the edge of an await-ing pit.

For one breathless moment Michael held his foe high above his head.

The gurgling pit bellowed its invitation. With that, Michael hurled the crushed serpent into the bowels of everlasting perdition.

Men and angels found no voice, that is, not until a most amazing spectacle appeared beside the froth-ing pit.

CHAPTER
Twenty

"What is that?" asked a stunned Adorae.

"Whatever it is, look beside it. The hideous thing lies next to a grave," added Gloir in repulsion.

"Not *a* grave," answered Recorder. "It is *the* grave. The grave which contains all graves. The cemetery of all graves!"

"*The* grave? What do you mean?" urged Rathel, not taking his eyes off the horrid form lying beside the pit.

"*That* is the grave of your Lord! All other graves are in it. Within that grave lies the final resting place of all creation, *and* all slavery to all works and deeds. In that grave is everything that is fallen. In it lies all creation and all its contents. All these were inside the Lord when his body was laid into *that* grave."

"Look!" exclaimed Adorae.

The young Carpenter strode over to the foreboding corpse.

"What is that heinous thing? Of what interest is it to our Lord?" asked Adorae again.

"Death!" cried the Lord, speaking to the corpse.

Shocked at such a disclosure, the angels recoiled.

"Azell! The enemy of God, here? Why is that seraphic monster present?" fumed Rathel.

"Death," cried the Lord again.

Azell did not move.

"Death, are you dead?" queried the Carpenter.

"Rise, you who once existed but never were alive. Or are you forever dead?

"Rise, O Death!" taunted the Lord.

The awful thing still did not move.

"The audacity of God!" thought Recorder. "Truly here is one confident of himself. And his works!"

"O Death, you who were the *only* enemy of God, where is your victory? You who boasted of your undefeatable power, where is your triumph over *me?* You vowed to sting me with your venom and hold me forever in your still and silent chambers.

"Know this, O Death, those dark chambers which once you owned, chambers filled with prey which you boasted were yours forever . . . hear me, Death: Those chambers are empty now. All of them. Empty! The prisoners of your domain are prisoners no more. *Nor were they dead.* They whom you thought were forever dead did but *sleep.* Learn, O Death, that there is but *one* who is *dead.* One, and only one! There is but one corpse in all universal realms!

Death, alone, is dead.

"Death, where is that victory? Death, where is your sting?"

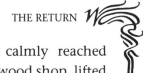

The Carpenter from Nazareth calmly reached down, and with strength born of a wood shop, lifted Death above his head and unceremoniously hurled him into the fiery pit.

No more is there
the enemy of God.
No more sorrow.
No more death.

Men and angels cheered and cheered, again and again, even as they wiped from their faces the last tears of sorrow ever to be known.

As they cheered, the Lord turned and faced the grave.

"Rise, principalities. Rise, Sabbath. Rise again, old earth and old heavens."

The Carpenter gritted his teeth in anger. "Rise, *law*, if you can!

"Rise, religion, ritual, and ordinances, you who stole freedom from those who are ever free. Rise now from this grave or forever be vanquished. In your place will utter freedom forever reign!"

A heart-stopping moment ensued. Then the man from Galilee raised the grave above his head and plunged it deep into the sulfuric pit.

I finished all things
before I created all things.
Now is that story ended.

*Now are all things old
concluded.*

Michael stepped out from the angelic throng, raised his massive sword above his head, and hurled it high into the vast oblivion of nothingness.

Gabriel, following, raised his mighty trumpet above his head. "Naught of the future requires the services of such a sound." With that, Gabriel hurled his trumpet in pursuit of Michael's sword. An acclamation of approval arose from the redeemed.

Urged on by such a witness, there followed the sound of ten thousand upon ten thousand scabbards falling from the waists of angels. A hundred million angels swung their swords for the last time as they cast them into the vortex of nothingness.

With that, the faithful Recorder rose before his Lord.

*Oh, you who are forever Alpha
yet forever Omega—
as you stood
at the beginning,
at that same
moment
you stood here
at the end
and saw these
who are redeemed here.
It was at the end
the names*

of those
whom your Father
gave to you
were placed
into the Book of Life.

With those words spoken, the Lord Jesus handed
to Recorder the very Book of Life, its pages all blank.

Today I write
those names
and hurl the
Book of Life
back to
the beginning—
back to you,
for you always
are
at the beginning
and always are at the end.
Two places where you always are.
The beginning
so long past,
nonetheless
awaits the moment
you will hand to me
the Book of Life!
Those whom you see
here
at the end,

your chosen ones,
their names I write.
Here, now, I fill the Book.
Oh, Omega,
there, at the beginning,
you will place
this same Book
into my ignorant hands.
There shall I peer
into its pages
not knowing how these names
came to be inscribed
even
before creation.
But now I know.
I look about and see
those who are redeemed!
And now, at the end,
with my own hand
I fill the
Book of Life
with the names of those
who made it here.

Recorder looked about. In a flash the Book of Life was filled. Recorder then threw the completed Book back through time, back through all recorded history, back to the beginning of a creation that no longer existed, backward through space-time that no longer is, until the Book of Life arrived into the hands of the Lord at the moment when he began to create.

At that moment, a scene from ancient past now unfolded before the delighted eyes of the multitude of angels. They watched with joy and honor as the Lord placed the Book of Life into the hands of a newly created angel named Recorder. With childlike delight they continued to watch as they saw Recorder open the Book of Life and, in amazement, ask his Lord from whence came all these names.

"Lord, whose names are these?" they heard Recorder say! "There are none living except you and your servant. Nor have I lived but for one short moment, yet this book so full of names has been recorded in *my* handwriting!"

"So that is what happened at the beginning of the Beginning," breathed Michael. "Truly all creation is in him. Therefore he must, at once, be both Beginning and End. All things are enveloped in our Lord. He is always at the beginning and at the end."

The ancient scene of long past vanished.

The respectful eyes of angels all turned to Recorder.

"My stewardship is ended," he announced in grand relief. Then he turned and faced his Lord, laying at his feet the blazing pen of gold, along with the other book, the Book of Records.

"Well done, most faithful of all servants," said the Lord as he drew Recorder into his embrace. Recorder buried his face within the arms of his Lord, as both broke into tears.

Michael and Gabriel rose and circled above them. As they did, the Lord signaled for them to join him.

Two archangels, the recording angel, and the Lord of all locked one another in full embrace.

The Lord raised one hand above his head and declared in exhilarated delight,

Go now,
Recorder.
At last
join your companions.

The angels broke out into wild applause as they opened a royal path through their midst. Recorder passed in among his fellows with ebullient shouts of praise as he found himself, for the first time, a comrade in the ranks of angels.

"Forevermore!" cried the angels. "Now is Recorder among us, forevermore!"

Recorder, ever the faithful steward, made his way toward Michael. Pulling the archangel close to him, Recorder whispered hoarsely, "In a moment we shall all witness the *second* beginning. The first was witnessed only by me. This beginning will be seen by all!"

CHAPTER
Twenty-One

Recorder raised first his hand, then his voice, his words causing the angels to remember something they had long since forgotten.

"We have a visitor among us, a man—a man who was allowed to come here from out of the ancient past. He came into the heavens. Do you recall? I speak of the prisoner of Patmos. Our Lord allowed him to witness many things—things that took place during his own time, things in his near future, and things in a future so far distant not one of us here has ever seen or ever known.

"But John saw. He saw this very moment long, long ago. He saw the *now!* He saw this day from heaven's view. He saw this day that he might report words of encouragement to those believers who were living in his time . . . and for other believers who would live in the times that were to come.

"That visitor, who lived so long ago, on an earth that has now vanished . . . he saw *us* here."

Michael blinked. "It is not easy to understand how one who died long ago is even now looking at us and beholding this moment." He shook his head, then laughed. "John, living in his own era, saw this hour before we did?"

Recorder pointed toward John and announced, "Behold the prisoner of Patmos. From millennia past he views us here!"

Sure enough, far below the grand gathering could be seen the ancient John, standing on Mount Patmos peering through an open Door, beholding times and places that had not yet occurred.

"Why is he not now looking toward us, Gabriel?" inquired Exalta.

"I do not know, but I am certain he does not see us. But—"

"I believe we would all be wise to look in the direction John is facing," Michael interrupted, "for your Lord has also turned in that direction. Surely, something astounding is about to happen."

"How do you know?" asked Gabriel edgedly.

"Easy enough," said Michael. "Recorder just told me!"

PART

V

CHAPTER
Twenty-Two

John stood on the Isle of Patmos, straining to see what might next unfold.

"I must write all this down. I must remember. I must. For the assemblies. The assembled ones in each city must know these things. What comfort there is in these revealings. Not only for the gatherings *now,* but for those yet to come—for all the assemblies of all the ages. How comforted they will be to learn the certainty of these wondrous events."

Behind John, but unknown to him, stood the citizenry of a former heaven as well as those of a former earth; and standing in their midst, the God-Man. All their eyes—as one—were riveted on that empty space where the Lord and John were looking.

"Our Lord is about to create . . . again. I see it in his eyes. It will be as before. A new creation flowing forth," said Recorder.

The Lord raised his hands, lifting both above his head. From out of the Lord's *bosom* began to flow a river of sparkling, whirling light that cascaded out into the vast void.

This emission of light, flooding out into nothing, began to wind itself into a sphere. As the light of the glistening sphere grew, all eyes strained to see something that was embedded within.

A new heaven
far more beautiful
than before

"It is . . . it is as if it were alive," exclaimed the amazed Recorder. "Nor is this creation anything akin to what I expected. Oh, the poor imagination of a mere angel."

Again a stream of sparkling light, like living starfire, pouring out of the bosom of the Lord Jesus, swept into space and curled itself into a glistening sphere. In a moment there emerged within the fiery light a new earth.

"It *is* alive!" exclaimed an even more startled Recorder.

"A planet pulsating with life . . . alive . . . coming from out of his very being. What creation is this? The new heavens are more beautiful than ever were the old. The new earth is more beautiful than both the former heaven and the former earth. And something of his being woven into their very being. Further, they live!"

An aged fisherman, living in a century that had passed away thousands of years previously, stared at the same sight and cried aloud,

I see
a new heaven
and
a new earth.
The former heaven
and
the former earth
have
passed away.

The two new spheres, visible, yet of the invisibles, began to move toward one another. The eyes of the old apostle shined with wonder and tears as he whispered to himself,

All
of the old
has
passed away.

John then heard a voice. So also did the angels. It was Recorder.

"Who has the right to rule the new *heavens?* Who, among heaven's own, is of such royal blood?"

Recorder paused and awaited an answer.

There was silence. Recorder called out again. "Who, among earthen citizens, is able to rule the new earth? Who, among earth's own, is of such royal blood?"

It was Michael who spoke for the angels.

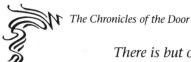

*There is but one who is worthy
to sit upon the throne
of
the new heavens—
he who is the royal Son of God.*

The angelic throng broke into wild shouts of approval.

Then, from out of the ranks of a new mankind, a man took his place beside Michael. It was Adam.

"Who has the right to rule the new earth? There is but *one*. A *man* must rule the earth!" cried Adam. "There is but one of such royal blood, only one who is worthy! He who is the descendent of a king, even King David. He who is the Son of Man is worthy to rule the new earth."

The ranks of a new mankind broke into exuberant cheers.

Together Adam and Michael cried aloud. "There is but one worthy to rule heaven. There is but one worthy to rule earth. His name is Jesus!"

Though the angelic host roared their approval, it was a new humanity that unleashed an even greater crescendo of praise. "Jesus is Lord of earth," shouted the sons and daughters of God. Then, together, the species of heaven and the species of earth joined in one voice of acclamation.

*Jesus is Lord of heaven!
Jesus is Lord of earth!*

Every eye turned toward the Carpenter.

"You are King of heaven!" cried the voices of man-kind.

"You are Lord of earth!" rejoiced the angelic host.

The ranks of two realms melted into one as a thunderous ovation (which only a new creation could have survived) rolled across the spheres.

> *At last*
> *you are Lord*
> *of*
> *heaven and earth.*
> *You are Lord of lords!*
> *You are King of kings!*

The angels rose above the redeemed and cried again, "Lord of lords!" The sons and daughters of God echoed back, "King of kings!"

Recorder raised his hands and began to lead the single choir in a grandiose shout of "Hallelujah!"

On and on rolled the jubilant choir. "Praise our Lord! Hallelujah, hallelujah!"

Angels, though not at all used to being out-sounded, rejoiced the more as they found they could not unleash praises and songs quite as fervently as did the sons and daughters of God.

Again and again this endless sea of men and angels caroled together in a harmony so fair that it joyfully broke the hearts of all.

Two innumerable hosts, blending the majestic

harmony of the highest life with the symphonic beauty of the second highest life into one enraptured song, proclaimed,

King of kings!
Lord of lords!
Hallelujah,
hallelujah!
For the Lord our
God
reigns!
Hallelujah,
hallelujah!

Adulation soared. Adoration ascended.

Still singing in union with their new companions, the angels formed a vast tunnel of swirling light around the Lord and his holy ones.

The old is gone.
All things are new.
Hallelujah
to our reigning Lord
who rules over all!

Michael, beside himself, rose above the gathering to offer a grand tribute to his Lord.

CHAPTER
Twenty-Three

"Not one evidence of the old, fallen creation remains!" cried Michael.

Just before the duet of men and angels could respond, a protesting Recorder called out in full alarm, "Not so, not so!" For Recorder still knew of things known to no others.

Michael fell silent, fully aware of the wisdom of his ancient companion. Angels and redeemed formed themselves into a great semicircle and awaited a further word from the venerated angel who had moved to the side of the Carpenter.

"There is, there always has been, even from creation . . . a witness to the existence of the fall. There is, and forever will be, a reminder of the price of redemption.

"You who are redeemed, behold your own bodies. Are they not flawless in every way, perfect in every degree? As heavenly as heaven, as spiritual as spirit, yet physical, in form, human? Your souls, are they not as pure as the purity of God, your righteousness as righteous as God? Your perfection, exceeding all

perfection save God alone? Upon you no spot, no wrinkle, no scar?

"Angels of light, younger now than ever before. Angelic glow brighter than ever before. There is no flaw among us. Yet, in the midst of all of us is one who is terribly scarred. That scar, forever present . . . present even *before* creation, as I am witness . . . a scar ever reminding us of our deliverance."

Recorder turned and knelt at the feet of the day laborer from Nazareth, the Lamb slain from the foundation of the world.

"Lord, that which you showed to me in the moment following my creation, I humbly request you now reveal to your brothers and sisters."

From out of the bosom of the Carpenter came a flicker of light. The light grew brighter, soon enveloping the Carpenter in golden ambiance.

Angels shielded their eyes while the redeemed looked on in wonder. The glory of the God-Man became a hurricane of golden fire. His garments, billowing in the waves of cascading light, revealed his side!

"The wounded side!" cried the ransomed ones.

"A scar upon the perfect one."

"The only flaw in all the new creation."

It was the provocation of this sight that unleashed the grandest song that ever shall be heard.

> *Worthy is the Lamb!*
> *Worthy is the Lamb!*
> *Alpha is and Omega is*

the triumphant Lamb
who
for the redeemed
was
slain.
Out of his side,
the crimson blood.
Out of his side,
the
perfect Bride.

You are worthy,
worthy to receive
all glory!

Spontaneously the elect reached above their heads, grasped their crowns, and cast them at the feet of their Lord.

Worthy,
O Lamb,
are you.
Receive all honor.
Receive all glory.
Receive all praise.
Now are all things
for your glory.
You are worthy,
O Lord!

All races, kinds, and kin fell on their faces and worshiped him who is worthy of all worship.

And yet John, peering into this supernal moment from another age and another creation, along with the angels and redeemed, was about to discover that it was possible for a yet greater scene to unfold before his eyes.

CHAPTER
Twenty-Four

"Now to your home!" proclaimed the Lord.

"Heaven! We are going to heaven!" responded many of the holy ones.

"This is going to come as a great shock for many of them," observed Michael. "Some of the holy ones are so intent on heaven as home they may find it difficult to accept a better place!" he laughed.

"Neither earth nor heaven is your home. Only two among you have ever seen your home. Come, Adam. Come, Eve. Tell of man's past and *future* home."

The first man and the first woman of creation stepped forward. Once robed in fig leaves, they now appeared before their Lord clothed in the light of his righteousness.

"Our former home, it still exists?" sighed Adam.

"It does," replied the Lord, "only it has changed."

"Will Adam and I once more be privileged to live there?" came the gentle voice of Eve.

"You and *all* the holy ones."

"And as before . . . you, also, my Lord?" asked Adam.

"Yes, as before," gently replied the Lord. "I, too, shall live there."

Adam turned and faced the great multitude of the redeemed.

"Hear me, fellow citizens of the kingdom of God. Created on earth, of clay, but with the wind of the heavens in me, I stood as a hybrid . . . elements of heaven and elements of earth were my composition. The home that was intended for me was—like me—a place composed of things belonging to both earth and the heavens.

"That place was the Garden of Eden, vast and beautiful.

"This garden lay midway between earth and heaven, *joining* the two. The properties of that beautiful garden were both physical and spiritual. That is, it matched me, as I was kin to both realms. I was part physical, but I was also part spiritual.

"The glory of this garden eclipsed that of heaven and of earth, for it contained both.

"It was within that garden that Eve and I fellowshiped with the Lord and, on occasion, also his holy angels. Clothed in light, we could see the unseen . . . ," continued Adam.

"Even as each of you are clothed in light and can now see the unseen," added Eve.

"That garden, a wedding of the things of heaven and the things of earth . . . *that* place is the intended abode of all of us who are gathered here," declared Adam.

"The garden was beautiful beyond words," said Eve wistfully. "In it was a river. Nothing less than the River of Life. The waters of the River were alive. But my words can describe the garden no better than my words can describe our Lord."

"In the river was gold. Bdellium, like pearl," explained Adam, then added, "and all manner of costly stone."

"There was a man there, of course!" continued Eve.

". . . And the man's bride," hastened Adam. "It was a vast place, as great as a subcontinent.

"I was that man, a *picture* of the man who was to come, even your Lord."

"And I was there, a shadow, a picture, of a Bride." Eve paused. "A Bride, and she is yet to appear."

"Positioned between heaven and earth, the garden was the center of creation."

"It was home," rejoined Eve, her voice filled with the longing of remembrance.

"Most unforgettably, the Tree of Life was there. Oh, how indescribably vast was that tree. The height of it? We do not know. Its crown reached far into the sky. Its ground roots, its vines, and the fruit on those vines stretched forth in all directions, even beyond the horizon. The fruit that was upon the vines was the fruit of life. The Tree of Life and the River of Life flowed together. The River, the banks of the River, the water, and the vine were always one, reaching out everywhere in that vast garden. Wherever you were, there was water and fruit from River and Tree."

"Most of all, our Lord was there!"

"In the hour of my disobedience, the Lord removed the Garden of Eden, taking it from earth. Eve and I stood in tears as we watched our home lift off the earth and disappear into the heavens. Since that day heaven has been the steward of the garden . . . that is, heaven has been the steward of our true home!

"Upon the departure of the garden, earth and heaven no longer joined. Commerce between the two realms ended. Our Lord caused a boundary to separate the two universes. On that border he placed one solitary Door. As you know, that Door was closed and guarded by a fiery sword and terrible cherubim.

A Man.

A Bride.

The Lord.

The River

of

Life.

The Tree

of

Life.

Gold,

pearl,

stone,

and

a

union

of
things
heavenly
and things of earth—
that
is our home!

"If you ever see these elements together again, know that it is *your* home. And the home of your Lord.

"I, the hybrid, partly of earth, partly composed of heaven, must have a home that matches me. But know this, our Lord is also of earth and of heaven. His home will also be composed of elements of both. He, too, will live in that garden . . . with us."

Adam paused. A smile swept across his face.

"Remember, holy ones, the life of God is in you. *You*, too, are part of heaven and part of earth. Expect your home to be as you are.

"Our Lord has said the garden still exists, only that it is changed. But you need not wonder if you will recognize it. You will know it instantly. Every species has its habitat; the instinct of our species knows its true home.

"The heavenlies are the keeper of that garden, but not for long. Earth is not your home. Nor is heaven. The purpose of the garden has always been to give God and man a home . . . *together.* In that place, as you shall soon see, the sons and daughters of God will, with their Lord, show forth their *oneness.*"

Adam and Eve stepped back and again disappeared into the throng.

All eyes turned to the Lord Jesus.

His words rang clear and with an assurance known only to God.

"The garden once wed the heavens and the earth, the spiritual and the physical, the seen and the unseen, making them one. Come, now, my brothers and sisters, look to heaven's portal. *Look to the Door!* Soon you will behold the Garden of Eden, changed. It comes forth out of heaven arrayed in beauty beyond beauty," he declared.

In that place
you shall be one,
even as the Father
and I
are one.

An old man, imprisoned on an island called Patmos, also heard those incredible words—and with the innumerable host of men and angels searched the skies.

CHAPTER
Twenty-Five

"Lord, let these old eyes see. Show me the end of all things, just as you said you would when you spoke of me to Peter beside Galilee's sea."

At that moment an angel took his place beside John.

"Let us wait together, dear John," said Recorder. "Together, let us behold this sight of all sights."

"You are the angel I saw standing in the sun. The one who guards the books, even the Book of Life."

"I am that one," answered Recorder.

"When I was young, my Lord said I would see . . . I would see."

"You will!" offered Recorder. "We stand here together in a place where final things are unfolding. You peer now into a distant future. It *has* been given to both of us—in this hour—to *see.*"

"What will I see?" urged John.

"Do you not know?" responded Recorder.

"I . . . I . . . He told us many things. But most of all he said he would make Jews and Gentiles one."

"He has done that, John."

"And . . . and . . . he also said he would make all of us one with him. More. He even said we would be his brothers and sisters, his kin, and make us one with him even as he was one with the Father. . . . *That* is what this old man wants to see! Will they . . . will *we* be one with one another, and then one with him?"

"Yes, she will."

"She!?" exclaimed John.

"Consider the word, John."

"Yes," exclaimed John. "Ecclesia, yes, ecclesia is a *she.*"

John paused.

"One with him! *That* much oneness? Union, even oneness, with our Lord? That kind of oneness is oneness indeed!"

"Come with me, John, to a high place. I will show you the Bride!"

"The Bride! Yes. *Ecclesia.*"

"You and I shall see her together. Come, for all the redeemed have gathered together, as well as all the angels. Together we shall see this wonder of all wonders."

Recorder took John's hands.

With the winds of eternity blowing in his face, John found himself standing in a space halfway between the new earth and the new heavens.

"Oh, I see the Door to the heavens. And it is open! Where is the sword and fire and cherubim? I can see right into the heavens.

"I see the throne of God. I *see* the throne of God!" wept John. "The throne, so bright it is the very light of heaven."

From within the blazing light enveloping the throne there thundered a voice calling to all.

"I *have* made all things new!"

John strained his eyes into the light.

"I know that voice! I heard it first in the wilderness of Judea! It is the voice of my Lord."

"On the day your Lord was crucified, standing at the foot of the cross with Mary, do you recall that you heard a most pitiful cry rise from his lips?"

John shuddered. "Yes, of course I do."

"I have heard that selfsame cry not once but many times. First at the time of my creation. Then did that wail begin its flight across time and eternity. I heard it again in the Garden of Eden, then in Egypt, then, as you, I heard it at Golgotha." Recorder lifted his eyes. "One cry, at last winging its way, even here, into this moment of the new creation. I will hear it now, for the last time."

The cry began.

John's nightmarish memory of that cry gripped his soul. He looked first toward the throne and then toward Recorder. Recorder was whispering to himself.

Oh, singular cry,
released in the act of dying,
heard even as creation began

again at the end
and now
at the new beginning.

Recorder was about to clasp his hands over his ears when he looked up in amazement. He could, for the first time, tell from whence the cry originated.

"Dare I believe *that* is the place from whence that cry has always come?"

Recorder straightened himself and raised his hands into the skies.

"I should have known. Yes, I should have known. That cry, it came from the throne!" he exclaimed. "Of course, it came from the sovereign, victorious, ever triumphant *throne.*"

Recorder strained to listen.

"There is no wail in that cry! No pathos. How can that be? Believe your ears, old one," demanded Recorder to himself. "It is a cry of purest *triumph*. It is the victory cry of the Lamb.

"Hear his words, one and all," bellowed Recorder. "John, angels, and redeemed, turn your faces toward the throne. Hear that cry. Nay, hear his words!"

The cry trumpeted forth from the throne.

It is finished!

"Oh, my God, it is over. Salvation is complete. The work is done. Lord, I am your witness to the birth of two creations. Now there is nothing but the new."

Recorder turned again to John.

"Now, visitor from times past and creation gone, let your eyes cleave to the new heavens. See what no one in the old creation has ever seen; then return to your time and to your people and witness to your world his triumphant victory, as I have witnessed that victory to mine."

John squinted his eyes. "Oh, Lord, let these dim, old eyes *see!* Then let me live that I might tell my people of this day and what has been proclaimed here in a new creation . . . that my Lord has finished his work, and is triumphant over all."

John fastened his eyes on the open Door. "Now, Lord, show me that garden! No, show me that girl who is to be utterly one with you."

CHAPTER
Twenty-Six

"Look there, angel, something is coming out of that open Door. What is it? Oh, whatever it is, it is glorious. How shall I ever describe these things to the people of my day?!" cried John.

"I see it! Lord! I, John . . . see . . . ! But what do I see? I think I see God's people? Is it your holy ones surrounding you before your throne, you in their midst? What do I see? My sight is made unsure by glory. Are the holy ones descending from out of the heavens? And with them the throne? But is not God's throne always in the heavens? And his people also?"

"There is a better place than the heavens for both throne and people," replied Recorder.

"It is changing!" cried John again. "Or am I but seeing it more clearly? Are my eyes deceiving me? Is it possible that . . . ?"

"What do you see, John?" urged Recorder.

"I cannot tell. The glory is too great," protested John.

"No!" cried John in unbelief. "Can it be? Has my Lord allowed his servant to see . . . ?"

"What, John, what do you see?" replied Recorder.

"The New Jerusalem! I see the *New* Jerusalem.

"I, John, see! Greater than all glories of heaven. Fairer than all the glories of the new earth, I see the New Jerusalem . . . departing the heavenlies and moving. But where is it moving?"

"You will know in a moment," sighed an equally awed Recorder.

"I see! I see the New Jerusalem *coming out of heaven.* I can see into the city. And I see the Tree of Life.

"Oh . . . ! Why, it is a *vine* tree!" exclaimed John.

"As the tree and the river once spread out all over across the Garden of Eden, so now that same tree and that same river find their way throughout all the city," observed Recorder.

"Its fruit is everywhere. And gold, and pearl, and costly stone," whispered John. "Oh, angel of God, look with me. I see the River of Life! It is alive. And clear as crystal. Look, the throne! The throne of God in the center of the city. And a man!

"The tree? The river? The throne? But tell me, Keeper of the Books, do these not belong to *the Garden of Eden,* the home of man before the fall?"

"This *is* the garden," replied Recorder. "The garden . . . transformed. The garden has become the edifice of God and man. The garden has become the New Jerusalem!"

"The garden, *now* the New Jerusalem?" muttered

John. "And the New Jerusalem, the home of God and man? Their dwelling place. No, our dwelling place!" declared John, grasping the moment.

"Of God and his family," resonated Recorder.

"The New Jerusalem has come *out* of the heavenlies. Heaven ends its stewardship of the garden," declared John softly.

As an ancient man and an ancient angel watched the New Jerusalem take its place midway between heaven and earth, John closed his tired eyes and let tears of wonder and joy flow freely.

"I, John, have seen the New Jerusalem, the very paradise of God. God tabernacles with man—and this time, forever! At last. At last!"

"John," prompted Recorder.

John opened his eyes. "Earth is moving! It is drawing near to the heavens. They are moving toward one another. No, they are moving toward the New Jerusalem. Shall it be as before?"

"As before," whispered Recorder, ever so faintly.

"Long ago, before the fall, the Garden of Eden joined together the heavens and the earth. Earth touched the garden on one side, heaven on the other side, making the two become *one*. The garden had in it the element of heaven and the element of earth. Even as the God-Man has joined God and man, so now the New Jerusalem joins two realms. God and man have finally found their singular home."

The two ancient ones stood in holy silence watching earth touch the City of God. In the same manner, heaven also touched the City, joining itself to the *building* of God.

"There at last is the City that Abraham looked for," said the two in unison.

"The home of God," said John.

"The home of man," responded Recorder.

"He did it!" continued Recorder hoarsely. "He has married the visible and the invisible, the seen and the unseen. In this City an invisible God and visible man dwell together. Seen and unseen, *one!* The boundary is gone. The Door is no more. The God-Man has made heaven and earth to be one."

So ends the chronicles of heaven.

"My Lord spoke plainly to me of this hour," said John, his voice shaking as he struggled to comprehend the incomprehensible.

> *The River flows*
> *from the throne,*
> *The Tree to eat upon.*
> *Water and food—*
> *in this same way*
> *did my Lord*
> *describe*
> *himself!*
> *And*
> *so he is.*
> *Behold*

now
a city
so transparent, so bright,
never is there
night
nor light
except the face of God.

Man lives
in the presence
of the light of God.
Twelve doors
all open,
and all are pearl.

Twelve golden streets,
yet all are one.

The light of God
is cast
upon the costly stones,
radiating
their endless colors
across creation.

The city
flashing its glory
as
one vast
many-splendored crystal,

clear as
jasper.

No death,
no pain.
The city's greatest beauty,
the living stones
and
the face of God.

No temple here.
The Lord God Almighty
and the
Lamb
Are forever worshiped here.

No sun. No moon.
The glory of the Lamb
is its light.

God and Lamb upon the throne.
The River of Life
and
the Tree of Life
flowing
together throughout
the
City.
We see his face
and

with him
reign
forever.

At that moment the throne burst into emerald fire, and a voice from within thundered its will:

Thirsty one,
come!
Hungry one,
come!
Freely drink of
the River
of the Water of Life!

I am your God.
You are my sons and daughters.

"What a sight. What an invitation. Someday I, even I, will be present in that great throng when all this does occur!" said the enthralled John.

The old man paused, then continued quietly.

"Listen to me, you who are called the Recording Angel. There was a moment, an enchanted moment, when that wondrous sight we saw looked not like the City nor the redeemed . . . but I thought I saw a girl. I thought I saw the Bride of Christ."

Recorder looked into the craggy face of the old prophet and replied, "It was as you say, John.

151

"Go now, return to the brethren in Asia Minor. Tell what you have seen."

John, the ancient alien from a past earth, foreign to so much engulfing glory, and staggered by the splendors of the hour, fell at the feet of Recorder. A stunned Recorder grabbed the aged apostle and pulled him to his feet.

"I have stood beside you only as a guide, to show you what will come to pass and what has, in the age I stand in, *already* come to pass. Hear me. I am, as you are, naught but a servant. Now, return to your age and write what you have seen; and worship none, save God alone."

The old apostle smiled, then faded from Recorder's view.

"John, back to his realm and his time. Lord, truly you are the Alpha and Omega. All things are *in* you as the *now*. You always stood at both the beginning and the end."

CHAPTER

Twenty-Seven

"Michael. Gabriel."

"Recorder?"

"You will remember that I told you there remained *two* great events *beyond* the Return. You have witnessed one, the end of an old earth and an old heaven, the end of the old creation, the birth of a new creation, the reappearance of the garden, even the New Jerusalem. You have witnessed two realms become one even as your Lord is of two realms that are now made one. Your eyes bear witness that God and man are together in their intended home. Two realms, wholly unlike one another . . . yet now one with one another.

"Still, all these events pale in the presence of what is about to take place."

"I cannot imagine," responded a bewildered Michael.

"Nor I. Not entirely," replied Recorder. "Do you recall just previous to our Lord's birth when you were about to announce to Mary that she would give birth from out of a virgin womb? At that time you heard your Lord speak of *his eternal Purpose.*

"Remember our Lord's words when he was a Carpenter? He so often said that he and the Father were *one*. Distinct, yet utterly one. The Godhead, so completely one, yet Father and Son never losing their unique personalities.

"Do you not remember that your Lord spoke to the redeemed, saying they would be one with him even in exactly the same way he was one with the Father? Can you imagine such an hour?

"'The Father in me, I in the Father; You in me, and I in you' were his words.

"In those words he spoke of the Mystery. 'Christ in you' was a promise to the redeemed. But so also was 'you in Christ.' It *is* possible that such things may be.

"There is a Purpose for which all things have occurred, *the* Purpose. The Purpose for which he created. The provocation of all events.

"That Purpose is about to be revealed, at a festival."

"A festival?" questioned Gabriel.

"Or, you might call it a banquet," noted Recorder.

The final hour has arrived.
The fulfillment
of
the Mystery
now shall be seen—
the reality of
his
ETERNAL PURPOSE.

THE
GRAND
FINALE

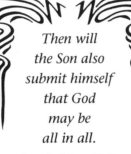

*Then will
the Son also
submit himself
that God
may be
all in all.*

1 Corinthians 15:28

The Grand Finale

At last had come the moment of the full revealing of the eternal Purpose of God.

The wedding banquet.
The consummation of Groom and Bride.
The finale of all finales.
The full revealing of the Mystery.
A time beyond the eternals awaits.

The redeemed from every tribe, tongue, and kin swirled around the emerald throne, lifting songs, praises, and worship to the Christ. Believers from among the aborigines of Australia, the islanders of Sri Lanka, the American Indians, the natives of Tibet, the Eskimos of the northern wasteland—all were there. One approached with hands opened and outstretched, another kneeling, another with palms raised high, another with face bowed low. Each worshiped God in his own unique way, lifting voices in every tongue ever known.

The light of their beings grew brighter and brighter

until that light matched even the grandest glory which the Son of God had ever allowed man to see.

The brightness of the Son began to ascend above all past knowing of light and glory. The innumerable throng, lifting one ecstatic voice in praise, drowned in immutable light until the throng became one with this brightness.

Eyes drowned in light, then became one with that light.

A throng of believers became one single fiery light. The Lord's final disclosure of himself had, at last, made the redeemed . . . *one!* The unveiling of the King had made the oneness of the holy ones a living reality.

This oneness began to change in fashion and form. Out of the purity and beauty of many who were now one emerged the fashion and form of a girl. Out of that light, which was now herself, stepped a being of such beauty that, until this moment, beauty of this magnitude belonged to God alone.

Her garments were her holiness, even the holiness of God. Her purity was that of the innocence of virginity. Her tressed locks black as a raven. Her youth as young as springtime. In her face and form was captured the rarest beauty of a thousand races of womankind. Her eyes blazed in emerald fire, her perfection, his perfection. Her features were the very masterwork of God.

Her beauty as terrible as the face of God.

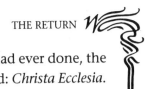

The provocation of all that God had ever done, the eternal Purpose, had at last appeared: *Christa Ecclesia.*

In you
perfect grace
and perfect charm
perfectly blend.
The face of God,
your face is
kin.

With heaven's light
your raven locks
are
strewn.
Your being
of his being
hewn.

His race
now
your race
is.
You are that space
that makes one the line
of
the life of man
and life
divine.

The sight of his scarred side would be her only knowledge of the fall. Yet, now knowing as she has ever been known, she recalled—in the most vivid of memories—that moment when she was marked off in him *before* the foundation of the world. Like Eve, she had *forever* been *in him.* As he had ever been *in her.*

"I, ever in you. You, ever in me," both whispered as they moved toward one another.

She had been hidden in him for all ages until the cross. He had been in her since the resurrection. Now they were about to become as they had been *before* creation.

All that was not the Carpenter-Creator returned to whence it had come.

So came that moment of final and highest expression.

Not union. Higher than union. Beyond union. *Oneness.*

The virgin Son and the virgin Bride embraced.

Utterly . . . *one.*

The moment of final disclosure of the Mystery had at last arrived.

As in the Garden of Eden long ago, when earth's first couple became one, now the Christ and his Bride became one. Kind of his kind. And life of his life.

Unapproachable light embraced unapproachable light. The Lord of all had won unto himself his perfect Bride. In that moment of brightest ecstacy the Bride became the wife. Two became one.

And love found its highest hour.

Now was Jesus the Christ all that was in that beautiful girl, and all that the beautiful girl was . . . was now in Christ. Her spirit, her soul, and her body, *all* permeated with Christ and Christ alone. All that was of her and in her was Christ. Two had become one.

Then came the great finale.

To the glory of the Father
the Son handed over
to his Father
all that which the Son reigned over.
Then did the Son
subject himself
once more to
his Father.
At that moment
and forever after
God
became
ALL IN ALL.

1 Corinthians 15:28

SO ENDS THE CHRONICLES OF CREATION.

AFTERWORD

So ends the play. The curtain has closed. Thank you for coming to the theater with me. You and I have seen a glimpse of our Lord as viewed by angels in their *chronicles of heaven.*

Will the players reconvene? Will there be more productions for us to view? Let us hope so.

I close by saying to you again, I am so honored to have been with you through these five dramas that have taken us on so grand an adventure into things unseen.

I hope that we shall meet again for other tales and other high adventures.

BOOKS BY
GENE EDWARDS

THE CHRONICLES OF THE DOOR
  The Beginning
  The Birth
  The Escape
  The Triumph
  The Return

Crucified by Christians
The Divine Romance
A Tale of Three Kings
The Prisoner in the Third Cell
Revolution: The Story of the Early Church
The Inward Journey

THE DEEPER CHRISTIAN LIFE
  The Highest Life
  The Secret to the Christian Life

Letters to a Devastated Christian
Dear Lillian
Climb the Highest Mountain

Gene Edwards's ministry
can be contacted at:
Box 18203
Atlanta, GA 30316

Don't miss these additional titles in
The Chronicles of the Door *series . . .*

THE BEGINNING   0-8423-1084-3
THE BIRTH   0-8423-0158-5
THE ESCAPE   0-8423-1256-2
THE TRIUMPH   0-8423-6978-3